Deep Water Tears

Book 1
The Dreaming Series
by
Jan Reid

ISBN-10: 0994248709
ISBN-13: 978-0-9942487-0-1

Cover Image by Mark Lucey © 2014 All Rights Reserved

DEDICATION

This novel is dedicated to anyone who has ever felt a sense of hiraeth;
a longing or yearning for 'home', or grief, for the lost places of the past.

ACKNOWLEDGEMENTS

I offer my heartfelt thanks to Steve Lennox, Christine Ramsay and my three (charmed ones) daughters, Tamara, Janaya and Cassandra, for your encouragement to follow my passion for writing and unwavering belief in my writing ability. You all contributed in propelling me forward to this novel's completion, for which I will always be most lovingly grateful.

Additionally, my gratitude and sincere thanks go to Wiradjuri elder Stan Grant (Senr), for authenticating and granting me permission to use the Wiradjuri content (dreamtime stories) in this novel.

To my trainers from the Australian College, Diploma of Professional Writing – Novel Writing and Publishing course, Dearne Cooper, Phoebe Hackett and Sandra Hisdoo; thank you for your positive feedback from my chapter submissions of Deep Water Tears. Your encouraging responses meant more to me than you'll ever know.

My thanks also go to Mark Lucey, for kindly permitting me to use his beautiful, timeless, Australian photo, The River Gum, for the cover.

Finally, but in no way least, to my Facebook friends - Thank You! Please accept my apology for not naming you all individually here. Most of you have been with me from the very beginning of my writing journey, encouraging, sympathising and applauding. You are the best!

AUTHOR'S NOTE

Although this is a work of fiction I have endeavoured to ensure the authenticity of all Wiradjuri (Indigenous Australian) content through careful research and validation from Wiradjuri elder, Stan Grant (Senr), and in alignment with the book titled, 'A New Wiradjuri Dictionary compiled by Stan Grant (Senr) and Dr John Rudder'.

The names, Binda, Jannali and Darel are the only non-Wiradjuri content. Binda and Jannali are believed to originate from the people of the Ngunnawal (NSW/ACT), and Northern Territory nations, respectively. The language origin of the name, Darel, though aboriginal, is not confirmed at this time of writing.

The term 'aborigine' (as opposed to 'aboriginal'), has been used to authentically portray such usage during the era in which the novel is set. No offence is in any way intended by such usage.

Please Note: All content (other than mentioned previously) is either a product of my imagination or used fictitiously. Any resemblance to actual persons, living or dead, locations or establishments is entirely coincidental, or has been fictionalised.

Hush now, 'tis time to sleep and dream secrets of long ago.' – JR

CHAPTER 1

Rachel leans back gently against the tall white gum tree and gazes at the shadows darkening the glistening river. The sun is beginning its descent across the water, but she knows there's still time. She closes her eyes and breathes in the fresh eucalyptus scent of the bush. Even with all the nocturnal sounds beginning to erupt and echo all around her, she'll hear him.

High up in the dark green foliage of the red gums the sulphur crested white cockatoos and pink galahs are jostling for their night time perches, and a laughing kookaburra thinks it's quite a joke. The smile that tickles her lips from hearing its laughter is quickly replaced by a frown of concentration across her brow as she tries to remember its other name and Darel's story about it; *gugubarra*, that's what he'd called it she remembers, and he'd said his mother told him the Wir-ad-jur-i people called the story - *a dreaming.*

"It's a story about how we came to have the sun and why we should look after the kookaburras," he'd told her.

Long ago, the earth was in darkness, and the emu and the bush-turkey were always being mean to each other, throwing each other's eggs high into the sky. The moon and the stars were the campfires of all the sky people. One day, the bush-turkey threw the emu's egg so high it hit some wood from one of the campfires of the sky people and the spark that came from it created fire. The fire grew to light the whole earth, giving it warmth and colour and became known as - the sun. After that, the sky people agreed to create the sun every day, as long as they were reminded. So, they asked the kookaburra to laugh every morning to alert them. When the kookaburra agreed it became known as a brother, and from then on protected by the people below because of its important role.'

"Just our secret Rach," he'd said.

Darel's told her lots of stories, and he's made her swear to keep them all a secret. She thinks about the time she had first asked him about it, here at their favourite meeting place at the bend in the river...

"Why do I have to keep your stories, secret?"

His usual relaxed countenance gives way to a rare moment of seriousness. "Just don't tell anyone Rach, or my Mum will find out. Ok?"

"You know I won't tell anyone. I keep our secrets," she pouts, but chancing another rebuff, asks, "But why does it matter if your Mum finds out, anyway?"

He squats on his haunches and picks up a stick, draws a circle in the river mud, contemplating his reply. "Mum said she learnt these stories when she was little, before they took her away and she got lost. She's never been allowed talk about 'em since. But she says she needs to tell me - before they get lost too," he ejects.

He looks up, his light blue eyes now welling up with tears. "I don't know what happened when she was little Rach. When I tried to find out she just said she would tell me one day when the time was right. But I don't think I want to know anyway because she got real sad when I asked her. She said something about 'sorry business'.'"

He stands, brushes the tears from his eyes with the back of his hand, and throws the stick into the water with all his might. It skims the water once, twice, lands in the middle of the river, and he watches it thoughtfully as it floats quickly away downstream.

Like many other children growing up in the Australian bush in the nineteen sixties, Rachel's contact with others her age was quite limited, until she was almost five-years-old and began her formal education. So, although Rachel Winton and Darel Rutherford were both born in 1960 and grew up on the adjoining farming properties of 'Binda' and 'Jannali' in the Barwon locality of central New South Wales, they were only vaguely aware of each other until they started kindergarten at Barwon Public School.

Those first tentative looks at each other on the school bus soon blossomed into smiles and saved seats for one another. From there it quickly developed into planned meetings after school at the dividing property fence down by the river, after homework was completed and before the sun set.

While Betty Winton was well aware of her daughter's wanderings in the bush and by the river with Darel, it was a double-edged sword as far as she was concerned. On one side, she was pleased that as an only child, Rachel had a friend who proved on countless occasions to be more than capable of keeping her from harm's way. On the other side, as she knew more about her next door neighbours, the Rutherfords, than most people in the community, she had grown more and more concerned about Rachel's growing relationship with Darel.

It was towards the end of their first year of school that Rachel and Darel were to experience the first repercussion of their close relationship and bring Betty's fears to light. It was from an incident that occurred on an afternoon parents were invited to visit the local primary school to observe their children during a lesson in the classroom.

As many of the fathers of the students at Barwon Public School, by rural occupation, were kept busy with the crops, livestock and farm maintenance, it was generally the mothers who took the time from their wash baskets, oven mitts and community fund raising, to keep informed of their children's educational progress.

If Rachel and Darel had eaten their morning tea that day instead of investigating an ant's nest in the playground, maybe things would have turned out differently than they did.

By the time lunchtime was almost over, Rachel still had a piece of banana cake left over in her lunchbox. She knew if she didn't dispose of it, her lunch box would probably pong of banana for the remainder of the week, and her mother would complain of the smell. It had happened before when the weather had been hot like today, and she didn't want to incur her mother's disapproval today, of all days. Today she was going to try very hard to make her mother proud at the parents' visitation day, and she didn't want it spoiled by receiving a complaint later about a smelly lunch box.

She had been about to dispose of the cake in the nearest bin when

Darel grabbed it and stuck it in his mouth, after having already gobbled down his lunch and a fairly sizable portion of chocolate cream roll, he had also forgotten about when studying the ants earlier.

The bell to line-up outside the classroom then rang, and with the excitement of seeing his mother walking through the school gates, his five-year-old stomach must have been fairly jumping around like a kangaroo, or *wambuwany*, as Darel would tell her when they were next alone.

A few minutes later, the visitors make their way into the building and assemble at the back of the classroom, to stand in quiet observance of their children sitting up proudly in all readiness to display their newly found knowledge.

"Darel, what is the sum of two plus two?" bellows Mr Glover from behind his desk at the front of the classroom.

No one heard an answer. Darel's face lit up, his mouth opened wide and instead of the expected answer, out poured a mixture of creamy brown fluid and massive lumps of banana. It was impossible to tell who groaned the loudest, Mr Glover, the visitors, or all the other children. However, what everyone saw without exception, and with obvious surprise, given by the looks on the faces of most of the visitors, was the boy's mother racing across to his desk and escorting her son hastily outside.

There was little doubt Darel's parentage was discussed in length in many of the student's homes that night, after it became evident the boy was Donald Rutherford's son. Gossip re-surfaced about Don, from

Jannali, privately marrying his aboriginal housekeeper after his wife's terminal illness had taken her.

From the time Vivien's health had first started to deteriorate, both she and Don had understandably become less and less involved with community events. So, for many years the activity of the Rutherfords had remained for the most part - out of sight and out of mind. If it hadn't been for the Rutherford's closest neighbour, Betty Winton, the Barwon community may have been left completely in the dark.

Apart from her monthly visits to Dubbo for grocery shopping and other supplies, Don's new wife Mary had rarely left the property, before or after their marriage; even Darel's birth had been at home. There were few people in the community who had ever laid eyes on her until that day at school.

There had been more than one visitor silently curious about the new-comer, when she had walked into the classroom. But, how could anyone other than Betty Winton have possibly known that the hazel eyed, honey skin coloured woman, standing in the back corner of the classroom, was the mother of the blue-eyed boy sporting a typical Australian tan? The fact that they both shared the same dark brown coloured hair only became apparent when they were scurrying out the door, and it seemed to be the only noticeable physical similarity.

Memories were scoured, questions asked and assumptions made. When was Darel born? Did Don Rutherford really *marry* this aborigine? If he did, it must have been because there had been a child on the way, and it was now quite obvious it was his. To think that of all people, a

Rutherford, would sink to that level. Poor Vivien, she must be turning in her grave.

While Rachel drifted off to sleep that night after having decided she would never let Darel eat her banana cake again, Betty finally hangs up the telephone and joins Bill in the lounge-room as he sits reading the latest newspaper edition of, 'The Land'. He is aware she is about to tell him why she's been on the phone for most of the night.

From what he couldn't help but overhear, it has something to do with Don and Mary Rutherford. Experience has proved that long talks on the telephone usually mean gossip is spreading, and gossip usually doesn't bear well for most. But he has no alternative than to hear her out, so he waits patiently while she collects her thoughts and begins.

"You should have seen the way they looked at Mary. You'd think they'd never seen an aborigine before."

Bill lowers the newspaper. "But Mary's not a regular darky. She's only half aborigine and a lot lighter colour than most of them at that. Besides, she's Don Rutherford's wife. Anyone from around here knows that the Rutherford family are the backbone of this district; the original settlers in these parts.

"Maybe that's the problem," Betty jumps in.

"What?" he's now confused.

"Well, people probably think Mary's still primitive underneath, and can't understand why Don would marry her," she suggests.

"Hmm, I guess we know better then, being neighbours an' all."

Betty sighs. "Yes, I have to admit, she did a good job keeping that sprawling old house tidy, and I don't know how she managed to keep it so clean. Everything was always spotless when I visited Viv in those last few years." She smiles gently, remembering, "Viv was so grateful. She said Mary had been the answer to her prayers, and she could rest knowing that Don would be alright when the time came." Betty feels she has assuaged her conscious now, and respected the memory of her deceased neighbour.

Bill gives her a sideways, knowing look. "Poor bugger. He had a lot to contend with though, didn't he? I reckon he knew the district would be waggin' their tongues about Mary after Viv passed, 'though I don't think he cared that much underneath. I dunno, what's it matter anyway, what others think? Mary's always been a good neighbour and she gave Don a son to leave the farm to, something to work for. Without her he wouldn't have Darel, and he's a good kid. He even looks just like his Dad, *colour an' all*," he adds with emphasis. What's it matter if his mother's a bit different? Seems to me, everyone should mind their own business." He scowls at Betty, before raising the newspaper again.

"But, it's our daughter I'm worried about," she counters.

The newspaper is lowered abruptly. "What's Rachel got to do with this?"

"Can't you see? *Everything!*" she gasps.

"Betty, they're only kids," he growls, exasperated.

"Yes Bill, but they spend all their time together. Rachel says she'd rather play with Darel than any of the other girls in the district. She says they're boring. It's *embarrassing*, and every time I turn around, she's taking off to the river with Darel." She sighs, "I still don't know what they get up to half the time."

"So, spit it out, what's *really* bothering you?" Bill decides to get to the bottom of it.

"Well, they're going to grow up Bill. Barwon's a small community. What if they end up, *God forbid*, wanting to get married? Because, what *if*, just say, Rachel has a baby that's a different colour? I've heard it can happen, a *throw-back*!" she exclaims.

"Aww, Betty. Seems to me, there's a lot of '*what if's*' there. I reckon you've just gotta let things pan out the way they will. Rachel's only a tot at the moment dear. Who knows what will happen down the track?" Bill once more lifts the paper, now covering his face, feigning indifference, although Betty has unwittingly brought up another subject he's been thinking about for a while now. However, he's not ready to discuss it yet.

Betty decides, despite Bill's unconcern, she'll not allow fate to ruin her daughter's life, or her own. He doesn't seem to realise that their daughter's involvement with Darel could have far reaching effects on them all. She is president of the Parent's and Citizens Association, secretary for the Country Women's Association, as well as the Red Cross, in Barwon. She wasn't about to jeopardise her standing in the community like Don Rutherford, because of Rachel and her involvement with his son. No, she'll take matters into her own hands, and promptly sets about to plan her daughter's future carefully.

The next day at school things invariably changed for Darel, and consequently, Rachel. Several of the other students made a deliberate point of ignoring him, as instructed by their mothers after the telephone party line had run rampant the night before, while Rachel's loyalty to her best friend never wavered for a second. If other students wanted to ignore Darel then they could ignore her too she decided without a second thought. Hadn't they ever pigged-out and vomited in their lives before, she wondered?

A twig snaps ever so quietly in front of Rachel, jolting her from her thoughts.

"I know it's you Darel," she whispers, testing.

"You're getting pretty clever Rach," a voice replies, and she opens her eyes to see Darel standing in front of her sporting his infectious grin.

"I thought you weren't coming," she teases, and takes off running along the riverbank, giggling. As she glances behind her to see if Daryl is following, her flowing light blonde tresses catch the last rays of the sun streaming through the trees. Darel is transfixed by the golden shine emanating from her hair, but quickly recovers when he sees a movement at her side.

"Stop Rach, *gadi, gadi,*" Darel yells, just as Rachel barely misses running across the path of a brown snake heading for the river.

She stops abruptly in her tracks. She knows Darel's never fooling around when he's uses the words of his mother's native tongue.

"You won't be going anywhere tomorrow if you get bitten by one of them," Darel chides as he catches up to her while watching the snake slither away.

"You know I don't want to go," she fires back, her emerald green eyes blazing at the reminder.

And just then she hears her mother calling from the house and sighs.

"I've gotta go," she says with a tremble in her voice.

"It's gunna be alright Rach," he offers as convincingly as he can. "It's only for a while. You'll be back."

"Yeah, I guess. But, I'm going to miss Binda," she says quietly as she looks wistfully at the landscape surrounding her.

The shadows from the river gums are lengthening. In the darkening light, she can no longer see the difference between the white-grey and red-brown of the trees hugging this part of the Macquarie River. By day, these trees stand like vulnerable, proud old men, battle scared bodies shedding the layers of time. They call them, widow-makers, without warning sometimes dropping large boughs with a *thud*, forever more lying in a prickly carpet of scrub nettle and spear grass.

There is quietness in the treetops. Most of the birds have settled now, but this is only a passing moment in the evening, just before the frogs commence their baritones to one another, possums hiss at intruders coming too close, and the murderous screech of the barn owls pierce the night.

She finishes her quiet reflection, turns and looks into Darel's eyes.

"And I'll miss you. *And* all your stories," she adds with a jovial smirk that doesn't quite came off the way she had hoped, turns and walks despondently away from the river, across the grassy expanse towards the house light.

If eleven-year-old Rachel striding solemnly off into the darkness had turned, she might have just caught the fateful words, whispered from Darel's lips, "I'll miss you too Rach. Binda won't be the same without you."

But, she didn't.

CHAPTER 2

Betty Winton closes the lid of the suitcase on Rachel's bed and clicks the latches into place. She straightens her back with a groan. That's it, all done. Now she can finally pour herself a cup of tea. She walks out of Rachel's bedroom, down the hallway, into the kitchen, and pours a cup of tea from the tea-pot, adding two teaspoons of sugar and a smidgen of milk from the fridge. She drags her heavy feet into the lounge room where Bill sits in his favourite armchair, reading.

He glances up at her, with raised brows. "You look buggered," he offers sympathetically, before returning his gaze to the newspaper.

"Well, I'm finally finished now, so that's good," she says, as she sits down next to him and lifts her feet up slowly onto the foot stool, carefully balancing her tea cup and saucer in her hands.

"Why wasn't Rachel helping you?" he says from behind the newspaper.

"She was earlier, but I knew I wouldn't get any peace if I didn't let her see Darel before she leaves. I'll call her in soon."

"Fair enough. What time are we off tomorrow then?" he asks without looking up.

"No later than ten-thirty, I should think." She gingerly swallows a mouthful of hot tea. "It usually only takes about two hours to Orange, but we'd best give ourselves extra time for lunch, and in case we have any hold ups. Our appointment with the headmistress is at two."

"Righteo, I'll be back at the house by ten for a cuppa before we head off," he answers, turning a page.

She sighs, deeply.

"It's for the best dear, she'll be ok," he soothes, sensing the worry in her sigh. He reaches his hand across and gently pats her arm, before returning it to hold the page.

Betty glances tiredly around the room, her eyes coming to rest on a framed photo on the piano. Rachel's sweet five-year-old face beams at her. She remembers taking the photo just before her first day of kindergarten. She had been so excited about starting school that day. It would be comforting to see even a hint of excitement about tomorrow. She doubts she will. So far, Rachel hadn't shown anything but disdain about going to Trinity, which had seemed to escalate the last few weeks as the day to leave Binda approached. Surely that will change once she's there she tries to convince herself.

She attempts to remember the first day of her own boarding school experience, but it evades her. She recalls though, by the time she and her elder sister, Dawn, had left Springwood Ladies College, they had made several firm friendships which remained with them as they went on to Teacher's College and successful pre-marriage careers.

They had both become teachers, although Dawn had taught at Bathurst and she had secured a position at Dubbo, closer to their family's property a few miles out. Learning to play tennis and ballroom dancing at Springwood had helped them find their future husbands too. She had first met Bill when he played opposite her in a mixed doubles match at a local social tennis event, and Joe had waltzed his way into Dawn's life at an old-time social dance in Bathurst. Yes, boarding school had been beneficial for her sister and herself.

She had always felt a little sorry for their younger brother, Neville, destined to remain on the family property. He had ended up marrying a local girl though, and seemed happy enough, especially now he had two sons almost old enough to help him. Such is the life of a farmer's son.

She blows on the tea in the tea-cup in an attempt to cool it down and sips it carefully. She glances at Bill. Several years after Rachel was born they had finally accepted there would never be another child or even a son for them, unlike their neighbour Don next door.

Even though he had just turned twelve, Darel already knew he would work alongside his father when he finished secondary school. Not that it would ever be something he would regret, especially as it was in his blood, an obvious tie to the land. Of course, he got that mostly from his mother, Mary, even though his father's family had been farmers for generations.

It was so odd the way things work out sometimes, she thinks. It would have played heavily on Viv's mind that she wouldn't be leaving a son for Don, and yet, despite all the odds, she had paved a way for it to occur. She was such a remarkable woman in so many ways.

Betty attempts to take another mouthful of tea, but it is still too hot. She carefully places the cup and saucer on the side table, along side her chair. She reclines her head against the back of the lounge chair, closes her eyes and thinks about her neighbours at Jannali, while waiting for her tea to cool.

***

In September 1954, Vivian Rutherford left the doctor's surgery and was quickly on the road home to Jannali. On any other spring day, she would have been smiling as she navigated the open road heading home. Bright yellow wattle bushes adorned the road side, a perfect match to the showy crests of the pure white coloured cockatoos balancing on the branches of the gum trees nearby. With the window wound down to catch the warm breeze, she would occasionally have heard the lambs bleating in paddocks, once dusty brown, now lush green. The rainfall had been good the previous winter. The land was now patterned with the green hues of the summer wheat and oats crops at their early stages of growth. Hillsides were bathed in the rich purple of Pattinson's Curse and yellow daisies, and the water in the full dams shimmered with the reflection of the sun's rays from windmills alongside.

But today, Viv didn't notice any of these things as she drove mechanically along the road in front of her. She had just received the news from her doctor that she had prayed would not come.

"The tests have come back. I'm sorry to have to tell you Mrs Rutherford, the cancer is too advanced now. You need to be prepared. It could be six months minimum."

Viv reckons she most likely hasn't absorbed the shock of it all yet, how things were going to be for her for the remainder of the time she had left. That was good, she decides; it would give her time to think more clearly about what she needed to do. She couldn't change the fact that she had terminal cancer, but she still had enough time to try to find a way to make sure Don would be all right. That was something still within her control.

There was no time for self-pity. There would be an end to her troubles, soon enough, but the effects on Don would be long-term. How was he going to cope with not only a dying wife but being on his own once she was gone? Jannali needed his attention from sunrise to sunset, and at times even well into the night. There was no way around that. The doctor said he would organise regular nursing staff house calls in between his scheduled visits, and suggested she consider the assistance of a family member or friend, until the time came for her to be admitted to hospital.

Despite the doctor's assumption that she would spend her last days under hospital care, Viv made it perfectly clear to Don, when she told him that evening, "I will not be leaving Jannali while there's still breathe in my body."

Don found that trying to understand *why* this was happening to his wife, the hardest thing he had ever had to deal with in his life. No, his wife didn't deserve to be dealt this hand; to suffer, God only knows - what, and fade away before his eyes. He had known that she had been concerned about a lump on her breast for a while and had finally undergone several tests, but *advanced cancer*? Surely there must be some mistake, he pleaded silently as his face contorted with disbelief. But, as if reading his mind, Viv calmly announced that she was not going to spend the remaining time she had left trying to fight a losing battle, and she would *not* allow her illness to interfere with their normal way of life. *Acceptance*, was what was called for, she said gently. Her time was to come earlier than expected, but that was just the way life often was, she had concluded.

He had never felt so powerless in his whole life. That night, he had lain awake beside his sleeping wife, tears falling quietly but unashamedly. The tears had not only been for his loss about to come, although try as he might, he could not yet even imagine his life without her. No, his tears had been for the courage he had witnessed in her eyes when she had given him the news; that determined look that he knew so well, which on this occasion clearly said, *don't you fall apart on me*. If anyone was going to meet this devil head on it would be Viv, and he could do nothing but concede to her wish even though he would have tried to move mountains to find a cure if she had let him.

Alternatively, Viv had fallen asleep quickly that night, because she had already decided that the only thing she was going to think about was to find a way to ensure Don would not be alone when she passed. She didn't have any family to even inform, let alone ask for assistance. She was the only child of parents who had been newly arrived immigrants from England in 1945, after the Second World War. They had both died within a few years of each other, soon after she had been whisked away to the bush by Don. The war had not only taken away their livelihood back in England, but also their health and any type of hope for the future there as well. Although constantly unwell, they had rallied enough strength to take the long voyage to Australia with their eighteen year old daughter in tow. But it seemed to Viv that once they knew she was settled in her new country, they had quietly given up on life.

Don had two brothers left, both living in Sydney with families of their own. As the eldest son, Don had inherited Jannali. Both his brothers had experienced the blood, sweat and tears lifestyle of a farmer and the sacrifices it required, without any type of guarantee in return. For them, a lucrative clothing trade in the big smoke offered a much brighter future.

Unlike Don, who had grown up in the area, Viv had arrived in the Barwon district and Jannali as his new bride after a courtship which had begun through her employment at his brothers jointly owned clothing store at Sydney. Their courtship had been embarrassingly short for a girl from England, but she had been instantly attracted to Don the moment he had walked into 'Rutherford Apparel'. When he had taken her to Jannali for a visit, she had no doubt in her mind that it was where she was meant to be.

She had warmed to his parents at their first meeting, and they had soon after welcomed her into their home as his new bride. However, before Don could even commence building the new house for his wife down by the river, his parents had been tragically killed in a road accident, so they had stayed at the original homestead.

It takes years, often decades, to build friendships in the bush, and even then it is usually with closest neighbours. Viv had no intention of asking Betty Winton for any assistance even though she was one of the few people in the district she could call a friend. She had no doubt Betty would offer to help, with all good intentions, but Viv would graciously refuse. She reasoned that Don would feel awkward accepting any type of help from his neighbour's wife after she was gone and try to manage on his own. More importantly, even though he got on well with Bill Winton, he had said on occasion that Betty often got under his skin, so it wouldn't even be worth considering. She could easily understand why Don felt that way about their neighbour, although she had always tried to make allowances for Betty's often undiplomatic words and brusque manner.

In the bush a man got used to working alone, but having someone to come home to every night took the edge off the loneliness of semi-isolation. No, it wasn't just about having a tidy house, clean laundry and food on the table, something that could be accomplished by day-help or a cleaner. She was looking for something else for Don. Something which offered him at least *some* type of companionship. This had occupied her mind solely until the solution had been found. They would advertise for a live-in house-keeper.

Mary's application was the only one of three applications received, which included an impeccable reference from her previous employer. Her employer, from a reputable farming family from Bathurst, strongly associated with the Anglican Church, made it clear that while Mary was from aboriginal descent, she was entirely trustworthy, held good manners and excellent housekeeping skills. Viv and Don felt there was no valid reason *not* to invite her to Jannali for an interview, pending employment. Besides, by now the summer of 1955 was upon them and Viv's health was beginning to show signs of decline. Time was running out.

When Mary arrived, Viv and Don attempted to find out more information about her, but her guarded response was almost a complete repetition of the information contained within her application. "I was raised at Cootamundra Girls Home, educated and trained as a domestic. When I turned fourteen, I was sent to work as day-help for the minister of the Church of England there, and then, when I turned eighteen, they released me from their care after finding me work at 'Baron's Reach', near Bathurst. I been there just over two years." There was nothing more forthcoming, but despite an ambiance of melancholy surrounding her, when she looked at Viv she smiled with such gentle compassion, they knew they had found their new housekeeper.

Mary worked tirelessly in her new employment at Jannali. From the time she walked through the front door of the homestead it was clear she knew exactly what to do. The once meticulously clean and orderly rooms had begun to align with Viv's ailing health, a sense of foreboding permeating from darkened areas, once bursting with activity and light. With Don working away from the homestead for the most part of each day, Viv had found it difficult to motivate herself to carry out tasks she had once systematically addressed each day, despite her determination to keep things as normal as possible. The cancer was beginning to take hold and spread through her body, stripping away her vitality. Mary set to work immediately to restore the home to Viv's satisfaction.

Her job description did not include caring for Viv, something which was stipulated upon her arrival, but that changed as naturally as the gradual transformation of the seasons, as the months and to everyone's surprise, years, passed. The doctor and nurse still made their regular house-calls, but it was little more than to monitor Viv's progress and ensure she had the necessary medication. Viv's and Mary's relationship quickly transpired from employer and employee, to patient and caregiver, and eventually, firm friends. Don was greatly relieved as he watched the transformation, knowing that Mary had become a good companion for Viv when he wasn't at home. He hoped Mary would eventually relax a little more around him as well. Although he was not a religious man, he thanked God many times for sending Mary to them.

On the night before she died, three years and two months after receiving the news of her terminal cancer from her doctor, while Don sat in a chair reading beside her, Viv looked affectionately his way from the big four-poster wrought iron bed, took a deep breath and announced as firmly as she could muster.

"You should marry Mary."

Don looks up with a distressed look on his face. His mouth opens wide; speechless.

"Now, there's no need for you to act so shocked Donald. She's already family as far as I'm concerned, like a sister I never had, and she looks after you even better than I ever did. You are still young Don, able to start a family. You need a son to pass Jannali on to. If it wasn't to be me, who better, than Mary? I know, like me, you don't care about the colour of her skin, unlike most people, more's the pity…"

"Yes, of course, but…," he attempts to intercede.

"No Don, please listen," she interrupts, takes another deep breath and continues. "You know Mary and I have become close friends these last few years, and I know a great deal about her than you will probably ever know. It took time for her to open up to me, and I think she only eventually did because she knew I wouldn't be around much longer to repeat anything." Viv pauses and frowns. "She's had a tough life Don. It near broke my heart to hear of it, but I'll tell you this - you won't find a more deserving woman anywhere in the district…even if you had the time to find another wife now anyway. We both know that it took a little longer for Mary to warm up to you than me, but there was a reason for that too." She pauses, and sighs before gathering her strength again. "We both know that trust, respect and a shared purpose is what gives life true meaning."

"Now darling, there's no need for you to worry about all that. I'll manage alright," Don attempts to calm her while still trying to absorb her words.

"No Don, I know you'll not want to remarry, but you need a wife and family for Jannali. Otherwise, all the hard work will have been for nothing. You know I read all the journals and family tree records of your grandfather you found after your parents…" she pauses, not wanting to remind him of their tragic passing, and changes the course of the conversation, "…I knew from the moment you brought me here that this house and land were special, even though I was a city slicker from Sydney," she makes a feeble attempt at a smile, but it quickly fades with the effort. She continues, more softly now, looking pleadingly into his eyes, "Don, please try to understand what I'm saying - once I'm gone, *don't give up*. You still have four thousand acres left. It was such a shame your grandfather had to sell off most of Jannali. Thank goodness he kept this beautiful bush home. We both know your brothers don't want anything to do with the farm, so do whatever it takes to hold on to it, keep it in the family." She pauses for a moment, emotion rising, "Oh, it just seems like the answer is staring us in the face, for both you and Mary. Don, please at least, *try* to find a way to love her and make her your wife after I'm gone, so that she has your name and knows this is her home for the rest of her life. God knows we owe her at least – that." She looks out the window at the setting sun, in deep thought, but returns her gaze to look imploringly at Don, who is still speechless, in shock by her words. "If you *can* Don, I know you'll both take good care of each other, and Jannali. Always remember, you have my blessing." she smiles weakly, exhausted from her long speech, squeezing his hand which has held hers from the time she starting talking.

After Viv passes, Mary grieves the loss of the one true friend she's ever known, but tries to prepare herself for yet another blow. Don awkwardly approaches her a few days after the funeral.

"Mary, I need to ask you something." He clears his throat.

Mary braces herself. "If you're gunna ask me to leave Don, I understan'. I know it don't look good for you with me livin' here, all alone," she says while holding back tears threatening to well.

Don feels his heart ache for this outwardly proud but gentle soul. "No Mary, I don't care about that. That's not it. I want you to stay. Will you?"

Don and Mary settle into an easy, comfortable companionship. Mary continues to keep house and tend to the garden, but Don often notices her walking around the property, watching him from afar. Finally, one night, she presents him with something to consider.

"You been talkin' about movin' the ewes to the paddock by the river?" she says while they are finishing tea.

"I need to finish sowin' the top paddock first though, before it rains." He yawns.

"Rain not comin' for a while yet," she states.

Don looks up at her intently, quizzing her firm response, but decides not to say anything.

Ignoring his questioning stare, Mary adds, levelly, "I can do it for ya."

"You know I don't expect you to work outside Mary. You do more than enough in the house and garden."

She ignores his words. "The dogs will be doing most of the work, and ya know I can drive the ute. Might as well put it to more use. Sides, I'll probably only need to open and close the gates. It won't take long. Save you the headache." She stands up and takes their now empty plates to the sink and commences to wash them without waiting for a reply.

Don decides she must think she needs an excuse to get out of the house more. What's the harm? He'll let her have a go, and sure enough, the ewes are moved without a problem the next day. After that, there doesn't seem to be anything she'll not volunteer to take on and accomplish, seamlessly. He discovers she has many natural instincts about the land too, like her uncanny ability to predict the weather. Most farmers look to the sky for impending rain, Mary looked to the ground, at the ants; watched to see which way the birds were flying, and the direction the wind was blowing. There is much more to Mary than meets the eye, he concludes.

Don thinks long and hard about Viv's dying wish after the twelve month anniversary of her funeral. Although he would have done anything for Viv, for the first six months he found it near impossible to even entertain the idea of remarrying. Besides, Mary seemed content to stay as his housekeeper, so why should he put a spanner in the works and spoil things? But was she only staying because she had nowhere else to go? What would stop her from leaving one day, out of the blue? After all, she was still young, and she would certainly make someone a very good wife, there was no doubt about that. She was now close to twenty five years old, an age when many women had a few children around them. As he starts thinking along these lines, he finds it difficult to imagine his life without her now, and he doesn't look at her quite the same way as he did before.

As Viv had become weaker, Mary had taken over as the silent backbone of Jannali, that's for sure. She had made sure everything kept running in the house so he was able to carry on almost like he always had. Of course, things were never the same, from the time Viv told him the doctor's news, but Mary had always seemed to know just the right thing to say and do, no matter the situation. That aside, she was also very pleasing to the eye.

From the first moment he laid eyes on her, he was glad they lived in semi-isolation. He could easily have seen himself needing to tell other blokes to bugger off and mind their own business. She was by far one of the most attractive women he had ever seen. He decides that Viv had known he wouldn't have even considered the idea of asking Mary to marry him if she hadn't given him an advance push, and although he finally plucks up the courage to ask her, he's now nervous she might refuse his proposal.

While he had originally thought Mary's arrival as heaven sent to help them manage with Viv's illness, he now sees that she had entered their lives for another very important reason. While no woman could ever replace his first wife and the memory of her would remain firmly with him his whole life, he had discovered that this attractive woman with her tall, slender form, honey coloured skin and wispy brown coloured hair had found a way into his heart, as Viv had hoped. These days, when she looked directly at him, and her gentle hazel coloured eyes met his, he felt like he was falling into a vast abyss of time, which soothed his soul and helped him look forward to the years ahead, instead of back in the past with sorrow. Whereas previously he had only seen the love and practicality of his wife in her dying wish, he now also saw her understanding of the woman he hoped would marry him.

Mary was helping him to heal, and he knew somehow he was helping her to heal too, from many things he still had yet to learn about. He was going to do all he could to ensure she remained at Jannali, by his side.

The private wedding ceremony led by Reverend Cooper of the Barwon, Church of England church, takes place at dusk in the back garden of Jannali homestead, underneath the sprawling purple wisteria covered patio and filling the ceremonial area with its intoxicating aroma. Reverend Cooper, although somewhat tentative at first about performing the ceremony in Don's garden, instead of the church, conceded instantly once he met Mary in person. His decision to go ahead with the unusual venue for the ceremony, he stated, with a condescending look, was solely out of respect for Don's parents and Vivien, who had been valued members of his congregation. Don hadn't cared less what the minister thought. He just wanted to ensure Mary had his name, legally.

Mary walks out the front door of the homestead, dressed in the smart ivory coloured linen skirt-suit Don bought from a dress shop he had found in Dubbo. Mary had not wanted to go shopping herself, so they had both searched through the catalogues Don had collected from women's fashion and bridal shops in Dubbo. She had turned the pages rapidly at the elaborate wedding dresses; instead pausing to look longingly at the skirt-suit with its rows of delicate pearls sewn into the bodice. Don didn't care what she was dressed in, as long as she was happy with the choice, so he agreed instantly. But when he had suggested a veil, she had looked at him with a stern frown and said, "What's wrong with my face? You'll be looking at it for the rest of your life, so there's no point hidin' it on our wedding day."

She steps off the verandah onto the daisy-lined footpath and walks towards Don and Reverend Cooper, casting a nervous glance at guests and witnesses, Betty and Bill Winton, standing quietly close by. As the ceremony begins, the kookaburras break into laughter from the treetops nearby. Don looks at his bride, and he is now glad she chose not to wear a veil, because the smile that erupts from her lips in joyful acknowledgment of the kookaburra's laughter will be stamped in his mind forever.

After a small dinner celebration, during which, to Mary's relief, Betty had monopolised the Reverends attention, the guests depart and Don retires nervously to bed. Soon after, Mary slides between the sheets and firmly tells Don, "I'm your wife now, Jannali needs a son."

Nine months later, the early morning chorus of kookaburras announce Darel's birth, along with the sun's blinding first light. His mother looks at his creamy white body lying in her arms and whispers,

"No-one can ever take *you* away from me. You are safe *bali*. And our totem, the kookaburra, is laughing with joy for us."

When Don asks her to suggest a name for their new son, she promptly replies, "His name is Darel. It mean - blue sky, just like his eyes."

***

Betty lifts the tea cup and saucer from the side table and takes a mouthful. It is now tepid. She takes several gulps and drains the remainder, rises from her chair and goes into the kitchen, placing her cup and saucer into the sink.

She glances out the window. The crimson hue of the sun is quickly disappearing into nightfall. With a heavy heart, she walks out to the verandah, facing the direction of the dividing fence where she knows Rachel and Darel will be, hidden from view in the evening light.

"Rach...el," she calls out. "Rachel. Time to come home."

CHAPTER 3

Mary beams as Don hands Darel the keys to the utility and says, "I think it's about time you learned to drive son."

Darel casts a big grin Mary's way, and heads out the door after his father.

Mary glances out the kitchen window, watching them walk together towards the shed. She hums to herself as she turns to the kitchen table, pours herself a cuppa and sits down with a contented smile on her lips.

Don had listened to her, as he always did. With Rachel heading off to boarding school today, she knew Darel would be feeling a bit down. When Mary had asked Don to find him something to occupy his mind, Don had told her he would take care of it. He couldn't have thought of anything better, she thinks. Darel's only just turned twelve, but a farmer's son needs to know how to drive. He'll be doing plenty of it before long, and he would be going to Dubbo High School next week. It was a good time to learn. Don's a patient man, a good teacher. She knows first-hand, because he taught her to drive soon after she arrived at Jannali. He's taught her many things, though he's often said it's the other way around.

There were some things she would rather not have told him, have him know. But he deserved to know the truth before she agreed to become his wife. Her smile gradually disintegrates, weighed down by the heaviness of the memory.

***

In January 1955, a few months after Vivian Rutherford received news of her impending death, Mary Gilmour brought new life into the world. As she gazes out the window of the train heading towards Dubbo, with tired red eyes, she doesn't want to imagine what her life will now be like, nor does she at this very moment, care. It's been a long journey. She should have slept. She had noticed the conductor keeping a watchful eye. She would have been safe. *Safe*, she almost smirks at the thought. When has she ever been, safe?

Through the window she looks at the flat plains dotted with mulgas and parrot grass, and watches the birds erupting from the trees in fright as the train barrels past, breaking the silence. Beneath an aging gum tree, a black crow pecks mercilessly at the carcass of a new born lamb, while its mother laments its fate nearby. "I know how you feel mama," she whispers. The hills in the distance draw her attention. A strange feeling of familiarity plays with her mind, yet she feels too depleted to think much about it. She just hopes her journey is about to end, before her eyes give in to the dead weights she now feels on her lids. The rocking of the carriage is comforting. It reminds her of a mother's soothing arms; a memory etched in her mind from long, long ago, and so recently rekindled. They took that away from her too. Once more, she weeps, until her eyes can take no more and close with utter weariness.

The carriage door opens with a bang, causing Mary to jump as she opens her eyes. "Up you get girlie, you've arrived," the conductor announces sternly, turns and leaves abruptly.

Mary tries to quickly stand, but almost topples over feeling unbalanced. It's only been two days since her belly's lost its weight, since her baby was born. She was still getting used to it. She picks up her small suitcase and heads out the carriage door and staggers, still half asleep, along the corridor to exit the train.

"You must be Mary, Mary Gilmour?" a stocky built man appears from the side as she steps onto the station platform.

Mary glances his way and tries to look at his face, but the glare from the midday sun is blinding her eyes. "Yes, I'm Mary," she replies, squinting.

"Good, good, I'm Don, Don Rutherford," he smiles broadly. "Let me take that for you," he says surprising Mary by attempting to take her suitcase.

Mary glances nervously around the station. "No, I can handle it," she answers.

Don is eager to get going. No use standing around in the hot sun, arguing about who's going to carry her suitcase. "Alright, let's get you home then. This way," he says, casting a quick look behind him to make sure she is following, as he strides off to the parking area at the side of the station building.

"Home," he had said. And he couldn't have chosen a truer word. Mary had stared out the window of the light blue HR Holden utility looking intently at the countryside in quiet reflection, as Don drove to Jannali. She had known he was appraising her out of the corner of his eye. She was used to that. But with Don, she felt it was more from curiosity than what she had encountered at Baron's Reach. She knew she was considered good looking, even by white man's standards. It was a curse she had to bear, being half white. She hadn't encouraged her last employer's son, even though they had said she had. She should have known better than to have told them he had forced himself on her; that he had raped her. She had been given a belting by the station manager for lying, and locked in her room every night after that, once she had finished her work. They had told her she was no longer welcome there and they would find her a new place to work. At first she was glad. She couldn't stand having their son, her rapist, watch her belly grow bigger and bigger with a smug look of pride on his face. He had even still sneaked into her room at night, using the key to unlock the door, right up until the night before her waters broke. But, that hadn't been the worst of it.

"Now Mary, it's alright," the mistress of the house attempts to pacify her as her baby is taken from the room by Mabel, another of several hired domestics at Baron's Reach.

"My baby, give me my baby," she pleads.

"It didn't survive Mary. It has no life."

"Nooo, I saw her. She's crying. She needs me. *Pleeease...*" she begs.

"Now that's enough Mary. You need to rest. You have a train to catch the day after tomorrow," the mistress says sternly. "You need to put all this behind you, you hear. Never talk about it to anyone, or we'll find out and you'll be sorry," she threatens.

Mary does not need to wonder why they took her little girl. It had happened to her. They had taken her from her family because her father had been white. And now it was her daughter's turn.

She had told Viv a few months before she died. It had begun to eat at her insides as she imagined the cancer was doing to her friend. She had needed someone to talk to about it; all the years of cruelty, despair and heartbreak - the sorrow of it all. By that time, even though she felt she could have trusted her with anything, Viv didn't have much time left, so she knew what she had told her would go with her to her grave. She need not fear reprisal as the mistress of Barwon's Reach had said.

By the time Don was about to propose to her, it was time to tell him too. If she were to marry him and have his children, she wanted him to know she already had a daughter, somewhere.

Just over a year after Viv's death, Don had said he wanted to talk to her about something. She had known he was going to ask her to be his wife. She had seen the way he had been watching her the last few months. He had always looked at her affectionately, but now she saw a different expression in his eyes. He was not like any other white man she had ever encountered. She knew he wouldn't do wrong by her. So when Don requested they talk, she asked him to take a walk to the river. They had walked in silence at the beginning, and she had sensed he was struggling to find the words, so she knew it was time to tell him what she had told Viv.

At first, she told him about her childhood; what she remembered. She pointed to the ground, at snake and goanna tracks, at the bushes with their wild edible fruit and those which were once used for healing. As they neared the river, she motioned to the trees, explaining how the various parts were once used for shelter and tools. She mentioned how some trees were important as landmarks and sacred sites, and when they stopped at the largest tree of them all, a big white gum at the bend in the river separating Jannali and Binda, she said, "This tree, the most sacred of them all 'round here. I know, 'cause my mother's people, the Wiradjuri, live in this part of the country a long time. You can see by these markings," she said, as she pointed to a smooth section on the tree and the circular, diamond and spiral shaped designs, cut deeply within.

They sat down on a log by the river then, looking out at the water, and she recommenced. "My grandmother and mother gave me memories of dreamings; they never die." She told him there were many dreamings, but she would tell him about the dreaming of creation, to help him understand a little about the spirituality of her mother's people.

"This the dreaming about the Great Spirit and Creator God called Biyaami. In the beginning, there was nothin' here on the land. It was flat as a pancake; no mountains, no valleys, no rivers, no animals.

Nothin'," she emphasises. "And it was very dark, no light." she continues, setting the scene.

"Biyaami, came down from the sky to the land and he made the mountain ranges and valleys, the rivers and the plains. He made trees, plants, animals and people too. He cared about everything and everyone he created, so he gave all the people laws to follow. He taught the law about looking after the land. He said if the people followed the law, the land would look after the people. He taught the people how to keep the laws, in songs, dance, and traditions. He taught them how to live. When he was finished he returned to the sky. He also called, Sky Father."

She turns and looks at Don. "Some of the minister's story at Cootamundra a bit the same, like about white man's God making the earth. But, there a lot that different too, like the minister saying when we die we go to heaven, if we believe in God's son, so it don't matter where you live on earth. But, my mother's people say when we die we become part of mother earth again; that when some ancestor spirits came to earth and finish what they came to do, they turned into rock forms, water holes and special places. That where all our family are and why it so important we look after the land; the country we live in." She pauses, considering her next words. "And that one reason why it so bad when they make my family leave their home, and then took me away from them too. They took away everything that matters. I been lost for a long time now." She looks back, trance-like, into the sparkling water.

Don had listened quietly, intently, to everything she told him about her mother's culture, but then she told him her own story; how the police had come and taken her away from her mother, her family, when she was ten years old, and he had struggled to remain silent. She had wondered if he had believed her when she had told him then about her life at Cootamundra Girls Home, because he had suddenly looked at her with disbelief, confusion. But once she had started, she had been unable to stop. The tears had welled up during her narration, as they had when she had told Viv, and when she came to the part about her rape and her baby girl, once more she broke down with uncontrollable sobbing.

When he had bowed his head, she had wondered for a moment if she had said too much, even to this man she trusted as no other. But then he had lifted his face to hers and she had noticed the moisture in his soft dark blue eyes as he looked beseechingly into hers and said, "Mary, I can't take away all that's been done wrong to you, but I can damn well make sure you'll be safe from now on. Will you let me be the one to at least do that for you sweetheart?"

**

Mary smiles softly to herself. Yes, Don's a good man. He had brought her home, as he had said at the railway station that day. And he had given her their precious son, Darel.

There had been no more children for them, despite their ongoing pleasure in each other on most nights, although Don was starting to slow down with his advancing years now. Mary giggles, remembering how he had puffed up with pride when she had told him that only having one child, one son, had nothing to do with him not trying.

Don and Darel were her family now, even though she would never forget her first family from so long ago. She had accepted a long time ago that she may never know what happened to them or see then again, although she promised herself that she would one day try to find her daughter, when the time was right.

Don had been her salvation, from fear, loneliness and despair. Darel was the sunshine in her every day. When Darel was a baby, they had talked at great length not only about what to tell him, but also, when. They both knew that when he started school he would soon enough be wondering why his mother was a bit different to the mothers of other students. And they knew it would be short of a miracle if at least one other child didn't point it out to him. It was something they needed to be prepared for, so they had agreed it was important for Darel to know as much as possible about both sides of the family, as soon as possible.

Don told Mary that while she had so much she could teach Darel about her side of the family from memory, he had his family tree records and his grandfather's journals, which included not only an account of his life, but also of Don's great grandfather's, Samuel Rutherford.

He said his grandfather, Robert Rutherford, had written that Samuel had been the first white man to settle in the Dubbo area, back in 1836. He told her how the Jannali homestead had been built four years later; a timber slab homestead, carefully and lovingly maintained and added to, throughout the generations that followed. He also told her that his grandfather's journals had said that Samuel Rutherford had got on well with the aborigines living in the area, from the time he first arrived in the Dubbo area, unlike many others who followed. It was written that he had even dismissed many men from his employ for interfering in the affairs of the native people.

"It will be good for the boy to know all these things, Mary; teach him not to pay attention to what others think if it doesn't sit right. That being different is ok."

Mary was much more hesitant. "Being different to you, not the same like me, but, you right, he part of both of us. Besides, it be easier for him, lookin' white and livin' in a white world." She was glad it was that way for Darel, although she knew it didn't guarantee a clear path. She had known full well what it was like to be different, to be the odd one out. Her Wiradjuri family had accepted her as aboriginal, despite her father being white. But it was a different matter entirely for the white people once she had been taken away. There hadn't been any sense in any of it. They said they took her away because being half white would help her adjust to the white mans way of life. That it would be for *her* advantage. Lies. Even if she had wanted to be part of the white mans world, it hadn't made any difference. She had still been treated just as bad as a full-blood aborigine by most white people; barely tolerated and with obvious disdain.

But, she was proud of her mother's heritage, and she wasn't about to let the white man win, completely, and Darel lose everything, by letting the knowledge of her mother's way of life disappear.

Mary had an attentive student in Darel, even when he was still no more than a toddler. By the time he started kindergarten, he knew most of the dreamtime stories and as many Wiradjuri words as Mary could remember. He also knew more about the bush than the average farmer's son.

"Now Darel, you must keep our stories and words a secret, for now. Ok?" Mary says as she combs his hair for his first day of kindergarten.

"Why Mum?"

"Because you have to, that's why," she says far more sternly then she had intended. She sighs, and squats in front of Darel, looking intently into his blue eyes. "It's just that most people don't understand these things and I don't want them giving you a hard time. 'Cause that's what people do when they don't understand something; they band together like a bunch of crows 'round a baby lamb, waiting for the first one to take a peck."

A thoughtful frown appears on Darel's five-year-old brow, but it is quickly replaced by a confident smile. "Ha, I'm not a lamb Mum, I'm the dog scaren' 'em off. Woof, woof..."

Mary had decided there and then, that her son was going to be just fine, no matter what life threw his way. And that was further reinforced once Rachel entered his life.

Just like Betty Winton, Mary was acutely aware of their children's friendship, once they both started school. But unlike Betty, Mary knew a great deal about what they *got up to*. Darel had not had to hide from

Mary that he had told Rachel about his mother's dreamings or Wiradjuri words. Mary had known. She often walked the well-worn track to the river and came upon Darel and Rachel playing together, without them knowing.

One day she came upon them sitting on a log together, talking quietly while gazing into the water. Mary had studied Rachel's delicately chiselled profile and discovered she reminded her of someone. Or, was it some, *thing*? It had dawned on her then that looking at Rachel at that angle was reminding her of a painting she had seen at the minister's home in Cootamundra. In the painting, the image of an angel was looking down lovingly upon a small white child.

When the minister had chanced upon her studying the painting, he had told her that the angels watch over *all* the little children. Mary had thought he must be mistaken, for she had never experienced any type of white man's angelic benevolence herself.

But now, looking at the sunlight glinting from Rachel's long blonde tresses, and the way she turned her head and looked at her son sitting beside her, she could almost believe there was an angel in their midst.

The minister had said that angels never die or leave you. She could understand that concept at least, because that applied as well to her mother's dreamings.

"Don't worry little one," she whispers, thinking of Rachel now on her way to boarding school. "You and Darel not finished yet."

Her earlier broad smile now returns, as she swallows the dregs of her tea, and takes her cup and saucer to the kitchen sink.

CHAPTER 4

"You will write a letter to your parents every week and hand it to me personally," Miss Bart announces, as the twelve girls sit quietly on their beds, facing her. Arching her right eyebrow for added effect, she looks from one girl to the next, to ensure their full attention before continuing, "And it will be a *happy* letter, to reassure your parents you are enjoying your time here." Pausing a moment to allow just enough time to quickly scrutinize each face staring back at her, she adds, "If not, it will be returned to you until it *is*." And with a tight smile, Miss Bart disappears out the door.

Rachel glances around, searching the faces of her fellow boarders, who are also doing the same. Most of the girls now look like stunned rabbits, blinded by the headlights of an oncoming car on a bush road at night. She tries desperately to regain her composure, aware her face most likely mirrors theirs. *Is there anything here at Trinity that's private or doesn't have a rule*, she wonders.

Too late. On the bed directly across the aisle, a freckled faced, red haired girl, stares at her until Rachel feels drawn to lock eyes. A smirk gradually erupts on the girl's face.

"You got a problem with that, *Bumpkin*?" she quips and chuckles. Rachel doesn't see the other ten sets of eyes immediately begin to stare at her. Instead, she *feels* it in the air, which right now, is thick with apprehension. She knows her reply will be an important one. It will determine her place not only in her dormitory, but most likely in the entire boarding house and school. If she lets her guard down and gives the girl across the aisle an honest reply, there will no doubt be snickering all around. She can't imagine any of the others willing to be the next target. She knows how it works, there's always at least one ringleader, and anyone who doesn't follow the lead usually ends up becoming the next victim. Even the kindest natured girls sometimes find it difficult to resist joining in.

If she could sense even the slightest compassion in those icy blue eyes now challenging her, she might be willing to admit to feeling like a bundle of nerves. But, she would never admit to anyone that her whole world has just turned upside down and she just wants to burst into tears.

She had been nervous all day, and her mother had made her even more nervous during the trip. For more than two hours, she had been stuck in the car, listening to her mother's ceaseless chatter about Trinity. She had *almost* looked forward to arriving at her destination, just so she could get some peace.

In contrast, her father had quietly navigated the familiar highway to Orange, seemingly oblivious to her mother's one-sided conversation, although she had noticed him occasionally peek at her through the rear-view mirror, with understanding eyes.

"Now remember Rachel, at first it will seem all rather strange, but that will soon pass, once you get used to it and make friends. But, pay attention to your teachers and also the House Matron. They are there to help you. Don't forget to pull your tights on slowly, don't tug at them. You don't want to put any holes in them with your fingers, but if you do you'll need to buy some more when you go on town-leave. Remember, you will need to ask the Matron for any money you may need. It's your own bank account, but only to be used for necessities…"

She waited anxiously for their arrival at the park in Orange, where they planned to eat a prepacked picnic lunch. Surely, by then, her mother would be all talked-out. However, her mother had maintained her monologue, even as they alighted from the car, collected the food from the back of their tan coloured Holden HR station wagon, and walked to a grassy area by the pond. At least though, to some relief, she had moved on to a slightly different subject.

"This has always been my favourite park in Orange, so many beautiful walk-ways, trees and flowers. Remember the times we've stopped here after visiting your Aunt Dawn, and Nana, at Bathurst, Rachel? Maybe we could drive over to see them, when I come to take you on an outing, between term breaks. "

She had been pleased by her mother's change of topic, and she had tried to enjoy the park, as well as focus on the idea of seeing her aunt and grandmother again. After all, it was always nice to see Nana's adoring smile, and that was a comforting thought. However, when her mother handed her an egg and lettuce sandwich, her thoughts returned immediately to the present. She already felt queasy in her stomach from nerves, and the sight of the sandwich only made it worse. But, despite stating she wasn't hungry, her mother had insisted she eat all her lunch.

"You need to eat Rachel. You may not get anything else until tea time now."

Her nerves were well and truly frayed by the time they walked up the front steps of the imposing two-story, red brick building of Trinity, to attend their appointed interview with the headmistress, Miss Pritchard.

They stepped onto a marble porch at the top of the front steps, where elongated gleaming windows stood either side of the biggest door she had ever seen. Looking up, she saw a white, cast iron laced verandah above. It reminded her of some of the older buildings she had seen in the main street of Dubbo. As instructed by the sign at the front door, they rang the bell and were shortly ushered through the door by a woman with black rimmed glasses and a pert smile. They were then directed to a long wooden bench, which reminded Rachel of a church pew, and asked to wait for the headmistress.

As Rachel sat between her parents, she noticed her mother had finally stopped talking. With some remorse at her earlier thoughts, she now realises she would have welcomed the sound of her mother's voice. At least the familiarity of it would have been somewhat soothing. When she looked sideways at her father, he reached over, patted her hand resting in her lap, and winked at her with an encouraging grin.

She tried to concentrate on a black and white, diamond patterned marble floor beneath her feet, but her eyes darted uncontrolledly around the foyer; at the high ornate ceiling above her, and the wooden spiral staircase in the far corner, leading up to the next floor.

Suddenly Miss Pritchard's office door opened, and the silence was broken by the sound of footsteps stepping from carpet on to marble floor. Rachel looked up and saw her new headmistress offer a final grin to the parents of another girl, then swiftly turn her attention her way.

"Mr and Mrs Winton, and Rachel, I believe," she then eloquently addressed Rachel and her parents, as the others walked away. She remained smiling as she motioned for them to enter her office.

Much to Rachel's relief, it seemed Betty had been preparing herself for this interview. She seemed to know exactly what to say, although the headmistress had seemed a little annoyed she had answered most questions directed at Rachel.

Once the interview was over, and they began the long walk with her belongings to her dormitory, she had felt her nerves settle a little. At least the interview was over and done with.

They were greeted by the house-matron, Miss Bart, as they entered the dormitory they had been directed to. Rachel noticed several other girls unpacking. Some were still with their parents, but there were others, including the red haired girl, alone. She had received general instructions from Miss Bart about what she needed to do for the remainder of the day, before walking with her parents to the car park to say goodbye.

Her mother held her by her shoulders at arms-length, to study her from head to toe, and smiling, said, "You're going to like it here Rachel, I just know you are. Be good, and if I can, I'll come and take you out on an outing in a few weeks." Then she pulled her close, hugged her firmly and kissed her cheek, before quickly getting into the station wagon.

Her father put his arm around her shoulders, kissed her on the top of her head and whispered, "Your mother only wants what's best for you, you know. She's going to miss you, and so am I. But, you never know, you might find it's not that bad after a while," he said, attempting to encourage her.

Rachel had then watched dejectedly as he joined her mother and drove slowly down the front drive, through the front gates, and disappeared from view.

Apprehensive about returning to the dormitory, she had stood at the front of the school, under the old maple tree, looking out at the distant blue hills they had crossed on their journey today. She felt numb, almost unable to move, until the sound of the bell ringing roused her from the shock that was starting to pervade her body.

Remembering Miss Bart's earlier instructions, she quickly made her way to stand outside the dining room with all the other students, until she was led inside for tea. She had noticed the red haired girl watching her at the dining table too, although Rachel had tried to concentrate on eating, despite again having no appetite.

Rachel can see the girl waits now expectantly with a taunting remark at the ready. There's no way I'll be letting her know how I really feel, she decides.

The last thing Rachel wants is to make an enemy, especially on her first night at Trinity. However, being considered a weakling doesn't hold any attraction either. One way or the other, she knows she's about to set the standard by which everyone will treat her in the dormitory, even though right now all she really wants is to be left alone, to figure out how to cope with the nightmare she's been dropped into today.

'Trinity, Church of England Boarding School for Girls', was chosen for Rachel by her mother when she had barely started primary school. Betty had been surprised by Bill's immediate agreement when she had first brought up the idea of boarding school. She had expected at least a little opposition. However, that he had left the choice of school entirely in her hands had seemed quite natural. After all, she had always known what was best for Rachel, he had said, so it stood to reason she would be the one to make arrangements. If she had wanted to start an argument, Betty would have questioned that response by Bill, knowing full well he considered her attempt to separate Rachel from Darel, nothing short of meddlesome. So, as she had attained what she wanted, without the need to fight for it, she decided to bite her tongue and put her mind to organising everything instead.

The only opposition she now had to contend with was Rachel's. But that hadn't shown itself at first either, when she mentioned it to her at the beginning of sixth class. She hadn't expected Rachel to be overjoyed to be going away, but she had anticipated at least some argument about it. What Betty was unaware of though, was that while she had been tirelessly enacting the final preparations over the last year, Rachel had done everything possible to allocate the impending event to the furthest part of her mind. And, she had succeeded quite successfully. That was, at least until a few weeks ago, when her mother had begun shopping and packing her suitcases for her.

"But, why can't I go to Dubbo High instead Mum?" she groaned, in an attempt to persuade her mother, again, a week before leaving Binda.

"Rachel, we've been through this already. Dubbo High School doesn't offer the type of education your father and I want for you." Betty sighs. "You'll learn so much more then education at boarding school. I went to boarding school. I learned how to be a lady and made lots of friends."

The case was closed - again. There was never going to be another opportunity to re-open it, because Betty promptly left the room and returned with a dog-eared copy of 'Pollyanna', requesting she read it before they left for Trinity.

Puzzled at first by the request, it had only taken a few chapters of the book for Rachel to realise that she was expected to find something to be 'glad' about, by being sent to boarding school. After considering it all, Rachel decided that at least she would be coming home to Binda for school holidays. That was something she could be glad about.

There had been a long day of shopping in Dubbo for clothes, shoes, toiletries, schoolbooks and the like, though, thankfully, she had been spared the need to shop for her school uniform. It had arrived as ordered, through the mail. Yet, it had still taken hours of walking down the main street and back up again, making choices and ticking off all the other items on the compulsory list supplied by the school. She had been so relieved when her mother had said they had finished.

Rachel had frowned at the clothes she would be expected to wear; gloves with her uniform, even in summer? And surely she wouldn't have to wear those tights, *every* day. She just knew she was going to feel strangled by her Trinity wardrobe.

Rachel wonders what Darel would do right now. Would he stand up to this girl, or would he just shake off her remark with a grin? He always seemed to know which tactic worked best at the time. She's not only learnt a great deal about the bush from Darel, but about people too.

This is different from Barwon Public though. She has to live with this girl; sleep in the same room, eat at the same table, as well as attend the same classes. She's even more confused now as to what she should do. Being called a country bumpkin isn't that bad she reasons. There could be a lot worse names, and she would prefer to be teased about growing up in beautiful Binda, above anything else, any day. But she has never liked bullies, and although she would prefer to walk away, she knows that's not possible for this encounter.

Then she remembers the day she had accidentally fallen into the river at Binda, and Darel had teased her for being clumsy. She had been so mad at him. She had thrashed about, trying to splash him, but he had managed to avoid her attempts. Then she had stopped, glared at him, and stormed off sulking. Later, when she had joined him again at the river, he had said, "You know, you try to look like a threat when you're mad Rach, but you don't fool me. You're like a willy-willy, going 'round and 'round in circles, chasin' your tail, and finally just fizzling out. I reckon though, you could be a real danger if you stood your ground and looked at your enemy dead straight in the eyes, instead. When you're mad, your green eyes are real fiery Rach. That's where the danger is."

At that moment, Rachel decides how to respond to the red haired girl across the aisle. Thinking about Darel's words, she somehow manages to summon up a confident smile, look squarely into the girl's eyes, and reply, "In the country, we like to *fix* things, *before* they become a problem." When she receives no reply, she asks, "What's your name?"

The freckled face girl's smirk disintegrates, as confusion spreads across her face. She stands up, roughly pulls the bedclothes from her bed back, and slides between them. "No problem, *Bumpkin*", she mumbles and turns her face away. Then she whispers, "If you really wanna know, my name's Mandy."

Rachel turns her gaze away from Mandy to see all the other girls look quickly away. She climbs into her own bed as Miss Bart returns, announcing, "Lights out. Good night girls."

Relieved by the conclusion of her confrontation with Mandy, she quickly gets into her bed and tries to relax. With the lights out, at least she can finally be alone with her thoughts. There are several enormous windows on two sides of the room. None of them have any curtains, but from where her bed is positioned, she can't see any stars like she can at home. She tries to imagine the familiar comforting sounds of her parents moving quietly around the house, but she can only hear the creaking of the springs in the beds of the other girls, tossing and turning, also longing for their own familiar ones. The usual lullaby of sheep bleating in a nearby paddock, which often helps her to fall asleep, is also notably absent. Those things that have always soothed her soul and made her feel safe. The things she always took for granted. Sleep is far from her, even though the day has proved an exhausting one.

The realization suddenly hits her hard; from this night on, and for the next six years, her life will never be the same again. Instead of waking up to the sound of her mother making her morning mug of hot milo, she'll be waking to the sound of the morning bell, and Miss Bart's doleful instructions. Miss Bart, doesn't seem to have a heart, she concludes. No-Heart-Bart, she decides to rename her. She tries to imagine telling Darel that, and making him swear to keep it a secret too, but the thought doesn't cheer her up. Instead, it just reminds her of how much she's missing Binda and Darel already. *How am I going to survive this place?*

Tears threaten, but she is acutely aware of the need to be quiet. She knows if she allows herself to cry, she will have trouble stifling her sobs. Instead, she moves down further into her bed, covering her head with the bedclothes in an attempt to block out her surroundings.

Finally, exhaustion overtakes her, and she falls asleep, dreaming of a long winding road.

CHAPTER 5

Rachel clips the last peg on her washing on the clothes line and glances over at the swimming pool. Two girls are doing laps, each one glancing at the other as they turn at each end.

It's nearing the end of her second summer at Trinity, but apart from school swimming carnivals, she's hardly used the pool. It's not that she doesn't like swimming. At Binda she would swim in the river nearly every day during the warmer months.

She sighs. "It isn't the same in a pool," she says out loud.

At Binda, it's only a short walk across the grassy expanse to the tree lined river. The water can be seen from the back verandah at any time of the year; sparkling like diamonds through gaps between the trees.

Rachel admits she's a pretty good swimmer, and she didn't need the ribbons she was awarded in the school swimming carnivals to prove it. She's been a swimmer ever since she can remember. Her mother had told her that she had started to teach her when she was only just learning to walk.

Betty Winton had announced to her husband, "I'll not have my only child drown in her back yard," and promptly became her swimming instructor. Betty then systematically taught Rachel how to float, dog paddle and finally enact quite a graceful freestyle stroke across the river. Back stroke and butterfly came quite naturally after that.

Unfortunately, as Betty would later lament, her foresightedness and back door teaching facility served more than the purpose of preventing Rachel from drowning. Once she started primary school, Rachel found a new swimming partner and a swimming hole, further down the river near the dividing fence of Binda and Jannali. This is where she'd be found on a regular basis in the summer afternoons, languishing in the water, floating tranquilly on her back and using her imagination to form shapes from the billowing white clouds in the blue sky above. Darel, never far away, would repeatedly climb up to the branch of a tree overhanging the river, and splash her deliberately as he jumped into the water close by.

How can a swimming pool replace that? she thinks, wistfully.

There's another reason she's thinking about the end of summer. It's her birthday on March 9th. She'll be thirteen and it will be the second birthday she hasn't spent at Binda. She's glad she's still able to see Darel on his birthday though, on January 19th, a few weeks before the beginning of each school year. That means she won't miss any of his birthdays. That thought cheers her.

Her mother had written that she would be coming to take her on an outing on the first Saturday after her birthday, like last year. She was looking forward to that. They would be going to visit Nana and Aunt Dawn. She might even see Uncle Joe too.

Her grandmother had moved from Dubbo to Bathurst to live with Aunt Dawn and Uncle Joe after Rachel's grandfather died. Rachel had only been two at the time, so she had never really known her grandfather. But she knew her grandparent's property, because it had been passed on to Uncle Neville, her mother's brother, after her grandmother moved to Bathurst.

Rachel remembers the trips to Bathurst to see Nana and Aunt Dawn, and sometimes Uncle Joe when he wasn't working. They had taken them fairly regularly; at least every school holidays. But, that changed after she started at Trinity. In the last year she has only visited them twice; once for her birthday last year and at Christmas. She thought that was really odd because she was now living closer to them than she had before.

She picks up her laundry bag and heads back to her dormitory. She wants to get back to the latest book she borrowed from the school library. At least when she wasn't attending to her chores, playing netball in the inter-schools competition in town, attending compulsory church or some other function, the weekends at Trinity gave her the opportunity to read.

During the school week, from the time of the wake-up bell to the end of - prep, the two extra hours of homework in the classroom after tea, her days were filled with bells tolling at intervals to announce the end and beginning of classes, meal times, piano, netball, hockey or tennis practice, or anything else required of her.

In comparison, she at least had *some* time to herself, on weekends, although that also had drawbacks too, at times. Time on her hands gave her the opportunity to dwell on how much she missed Binda and how stifled she felt within the confines of Trinity. Sometimes she felt like she couldn't breathe. There was nowhere she could go where she could really feel some semblance of peace. She couldn't take off to the bush because there was no bush; instead, there were only buildings and concrete, or perfectly manicured playing fields. And apart from birds, she hasn't once seen an animal of any description on the grounds, either native or tame. If it weren't for the common sparrows flitting from shrub to shrub about their business, she would wonder if perhaps there was a huge invisible bubble surrounding the school, keeping everything out, and all the students in.

When she started to think like that, she wondered if perhaps being constantly busy was the better thing, after all. That was, until she discovered a way to still feel like she was at Binda, without even leaving the school.

She had bought a diary when she was on town-leave last year. She had bought it with the intention to record her thoughts and feelings, but she quickly saw two major problems with that. Firstly, she wasn't sure she would feel comfortable letting her guard down, to write about her thoughts and feelings, when there was always someone milling about close by. And secondly, when she had imagined the type of thoughts and feelings she would write, she had come to the conclusion that it probably wouldn't serve any purpose, other than to make her feel even more sorry for herself. She had been aware for quite some time, that she felt sorry for herself. But, so far, she just hasn't been able to overcome it; even despite having read, 'Pollyanna'. So, her diary had remained relatively untouched for most of her first year at Trinity. However, one day when she was thinking with joy, about Binda and Darel, the answer had suddenly dawned on her. As it was those thoughts which made her feel happier, by recording them, she could relive them again and again. It was then that she brought her diary out from the back of her cupboard and began to write in the pages.

At first she wrote in her diary only on the weekends, but then she found she was even able to find some time to write before lights out during school nights. She even recorded all the stories Darel had told her, writing them just like she remembered him telling her. She silently promised him, she was still keeping his stories a secret. Her diary was for her eyes only, after all, even though there may be a room full of other girls close by as she wrote. She always made certain to hide it in the pillowslip on the bottom side of her pillow, *after* the lights were turned out.

As she walks into her dormitory, she's relieved to see that for once she is alone. *Bonus*, she thinks, but straight away, she hears whispers and giggling. She looks in the direction from where she heard the noise. It seemed to come from behind the curtain that serves as a cover for the clothes hanging area, along the far wall. "I guess it was too good to be true," she mumbles to herself, as she pushes her laundry bag into her cupboard, picks up her book and settles herself on her bed.

"Hey *Bumpkin*, what's all this gibberish about Darel and his stories?'

The book Rachel is reading drops immediately from her hands onto the floor with a loud, *thud.* She jumps to her feet, runs to the curtained area from where the voice came and reefs it open.

Mandy Morris is sitting cross-legged on the floor, holding Rachel's diary open with the thumb of her left hand down the centre spine, and smirking as she places a spoonful of Milo into her mouth with her right hand. The Milo tin is positioned between Mandy and her newly recruited sidekick, Chloe Osbourne. They both open their mouths, caked full of milo, and laugh uproariously as Rachel's face contorts in a mixture of horror and fury.

Rachel doesn't even care about the tin of Milo she bought on last town-leave and hid behind her jumpers in her clothes cubicle. Most of the girls in her dormitory had stashes of their favourite food hidden somewhere. But, her *diary!* Oh, why hadn't she locked it, made sure no-one could read it? If she hadn't been so worried about making a noise and drawing attention to it, this would never have happened. But there was no use berating herself for that now. She had to deal with the repercussions of her action, or in-action, as the case actually was.

She suddenly decides, as Mandy Morris seems so intent upon gaining her attention, then she would give it to her. That is, just as soon as she manages to find her voice, which just won't function at the moment, because somehow, she's forgotten how to breathe.

"Well *Bumpkin*, it's good to share you know, we didn't think you'd mind," Mandy sniggers.

"Give it to me, *now!* Rachel finally hisses through her teeth, hardly recognising her own voice.

Mandy, still smirking, briefly glances at Chloe for encouragement, but Chloe is looking tentatively past Rachel, as footsteps approach.

Spurred on by an audience standing behind Rachel, Mandy pulls a mock sheepish grin and holds the tin of Milo out to her.

Intent upon claiming her precious diary, no matter what, Rachel grabs the tin of Milo with her right hand and pours the contents over Mandy's head, while at the same time snatching the diary with her left.

Mandy stands abruptly, spluttering, attempting to remove the Milo from her hair and face as Rachel tosses the now empty tin to the floor. She turns and flees down the corridor between the beds, blindly brushing past several other girls, out the dormitory and down the stairs, clutching her diary firmly against her chest. It's not until she has made it to the far side of the hockey field that she stops running, sits under a tree, covers her face with her hands, and begins to sob shamelessly.

A few minutes later, Rachel is attempting to dry her tears and compose herself, when she hears a noise at her side.

"Hey Rachel, can I sit with you for a while?" Rachel looks up through her red eyes to see Jessica Hewitt standing in front of her with a concerned look. At least it isn't Mandy she decides. She nods, and Jess sits down beside her.

Rachel looks across the hockey field to the dormitory she recently fled from.

"I made a fool of myself just then, didn't I?"

"You really think so?" Jess responds with raised eyebrows.

"You really think I didn't? Rachel counters.

"You better believe it." Jess smiles.

Rachel frowns, bewildered.

"You stood up to Mandy and made a fool of *her*. And you know what? Because you *did*, you gave the rest of us the courage to stand up to her too. After you left, we all gave her the foulest looks, even Chloe walked away from her. Deb and I told her to clean up the Milo mess or we would tell Miss Bart she had stolen it from you. Even if you aren't supposed to have food in the dormitory, you know Miss Bart wouldn't approve of stealing."

"Ok.... I guess," Rachel tries to re-arrange her thoughts. "But she read my diary. How can I ever trust her not to tell anyone about what I wrote?"

"Hmmm, I guess you can't, although I don't think she'd be stupid enough now to risk you finding out," she says with a grin.

Rachel immediately thinks of Darel. "You sound a lot like my best friend back home. He always seems to be able to see the good in things." Rachel smiles at Jess, all of a sudden feeling a great deal better.

Jess smiles back. "Best friend or boyfriend?"

"Na, best friend. Since Kindergarten."

"You lucky thing. Tell me more..."

From that day on, Jess and Rachel became almost inseparable and Debbie Stewart, who had also stood up to Mandy alongside Jess, often joined them in whatever they were doing.

Life at Trinity was a lot easier with a friend or two by your side, Rachel finds out. She thinks that perhaps things will continue to get better from now on. It was about time, she decides. It had been a long and lonely twelve months.

CHAPTER 6

"Here we are," her mother announces as they pull up on the stone paved driveway of Rachel's aunt and uncle's cream coloured brick home in Bathurst.

Aunt Dawn comes into view, opening the front door, as Betty and Rachel step out of the station wagon.

Betty opens the door behind the driver's seat and reaches into the car. She hands Rachel a shopping bag.

"Don't look in there," she says with a smile, as she reaches in again and carefully takes out a Tupperware cake container.

Rachel walks ahead of her mother to greet her aunt at the door.

"Hello Rachel, come on in," her aunt says, kisses her briefly on her cheek, and gestures with a sweep of her arm to enter the house.

Rachel walks inside while her aunt continues to hold the door open for Betty.

They enter the light-filled kitchen, and Rachel looks out through the spotless wide window above the sink, to the back garden. Her grandmother is sitting in the far corner, under a shady, grapevine covered, pergola. She places the bag her mother had given her onto the kitchen bench and races outside the back door.

"Ahh, here she is; my favourite granddaughter."

Rachel's grandmother smiles broadly, places the book she is reading on the decorative wrought-iron table beside her, and opens her arms wide for a cuddle.

"Oh Nana, you always say that. But I'm your *only* granddaughter," Rachel responds, laughing and bending down to allow her grandmother to hug her.

"What are you reading?" Rachel asks, glancing at the book as she sits on the chair opposite her grandmother.

"Well, I've been re-reading some of my favourites. This one is an old classic, called, 'Pride and Prejudice' by Jane Austen," her grandmother says. She picks it up, places a bookmark carefully between the pages, closes it and hands it to Rachel.

"I remember seeing this one in your bookcase before," Rachel says stroking the embossed cover with her fingertips.

"Ahh yes, I remember even as a toddler you liked pulling the books from my book shelves," her grandmother says with an affectionate smile. "Although, most of the books I have left now were my mother's; your great grandmother's. That's why they're so old. Your great grandmother brought them out to Australia, from England. You were always fascinated by books," she says remembering. Then returning to the present, asks brightly, "Are you still?"

"Oh yes Nana, and Trinity has a huge library. I'm always reading; well, when I'm not doing other things. But I read a lot on the weekends. It takes my mind off other things, too."

Rachel's grandmother notices the sudden downcast look on her face. "Do you know, it's been over a year since we had a really good talk? It was far too hectic at Christmas when all the family were here. You were still only twelve then, but now you are thirteen, and a teenager of all things." She leans closer conspiringly, and whispers with wide open eyes. "Tell me, do you feel any different?"

Rachel giggles. "Oh Nana, It's so good to see you."

Rachel spends the next thirty minutes telling her grandmother a lot more about Trinity than she had at Christmas; the subjects and teachers she liked best, and some of the books she had read from the school library. When her grandmother asks if she has made any friends, she tells her about Jess and Deb, and even about Mandy giving her a hard time.

"It sounds to me like Mandy isn't very happy Rachel; it's usually the case when someone acts like that. Do you know much about her?"

Rachel doesn't want to talk about Mandy Morris. She wishes she hadn't even mentioned her name. But, it would be rude not to answer her grandmother's question, fully.

"Well, I found out she comes from Sydney. Both her parents are doctors, so they live in a really posh area. She talks a lot about her older cousin, and she seems to spend a lot of time with her," she pauses, thinking. "She spent most of last holidays at the home of one her friends from Trinity because her parents went overseas for a holiday. I remember her skiting about all the souvenirs they brought back for her." Rachel looks squarely at her grandmother now. "Well, I guess she probably doesn't get to see much of her parents even when she is home from Trinity, because they both work. She probably misses them." Rachel thinks how she has missed her parents too, but then a sudden thought comes to her. "It doesn't really make sense though Nana, 'cause I'm not very happy either, but I don't go around bullying anyone else."

Her grandmother reaches over and takes her hand. "Why are you unhappy Rachel?"

Rachel looks towards the kitchen window before turning back to her grandmother. She answers quietly, "Well, I really miss Binda, even though I go home for holidays," and looks down sadly, at her feet.

Her grandmother looks at her thoughtfully. "Well I think it would be a bit strange if you didn't."

Rachel looks up, surprised by her answer. "Everyone else

just keep saying that I have to get used to it. But I don't want to *have* to get used to it," she says softly.

"Hmm, well, that makes it a bit more difficult, although, you know, most people don't like change either? Especially *me!*" she adds, nodding her head as Rachel looks at her unconvinced. She continues, "When your grandfather passed away and I left the farm in Dubbo to live here with your aunt, I was out of sorts for a long time. Everything was so different and new, including this new house they'd just bought. But do you know what I discovered after a time?" she asks, and as Rachel waits expectantly, she concludes, "As long as I kept the memories alive, I never really left." And she squeezes Rachel's hand tight, nodding again, avidly.

Something then clicks in Rachel's mind; her grandmother's words having started off a train of thought. She was doing just that; keeping her memories alive by writing about Binda and Darel in her diary. Every time she read her entries, she felt like she was at Binda or with Darel. And Darel's mother was doing what her grandmother had just said too, keeping her memories alive by telling Darel about them. If she didn't tell Darel though, they might be lost forever, because they'd never been written down. The thought makes her feel sad, but it also makes her realise how lucky she is. If she wanted to know more about her cultures past, she only had to find a book about it. Maybe her fascination for history had a lot to do with knowing how important the past is, because of Darel's mother having to rely on her memory.

While she was deep in thought, Betty came out the back door to greet her mother, and they all went inside. Rachel's uncle had arrived home while she had been talking to her grandmother in the garden. When everyone had made their way into the dining room they sat down to eat the special Chinese taka-away lunch he had picked up on his way home from work, in honour of her birthday visit.

While her mother, aunt and uncle talk about his work in real-estate and how his business was currently booming, Rachel and her grandmother talk about their favourite foods, including cakes.

"Banana used to be my favourite," Rachel says with a serious expression on her face. "But it's now, chocolate," she says, thinking how she had never been able to stomach banana cake after Darel's experience in kindergarten.

At the mention of chocolate cake, the adults look at Rachel, and Aunt Dawn and her mother exit to the kitchen with the empty plates from the table. Her aunt returns, followed by her mother carrying a cake, covered in chocolate icing, decorated with pink flowers and glowing with candles. Rachel blows out the thirteen candles with gusto, and makes a wish. She smiles to herself, knowing that she doesn't have to tell them the wish she has just made. But, if it came true, her mother would agree to let her come home to Binda once she finished her School Certificate. That would be meeting her more than half way she had recently decided. If her mother agreed, she would only have the remainder of Second Form and two more years at Trinity after that, instead of nearly five. Surely, her mother would concede, especially if she did well in Fourth Form. She had kept her fingers crossed, hidden from view beneath the table, as she made her wish. She hoped more than anything it would help to make her wish come true.

After they have all washed down a piece of birthday cake, with cups of tea for the adults and a warm cup of milo for Rachel, they all move into the lounge room to watch her open her presents: a book called, 'Heidi', and a store bought white lace shawl from her mother and father, a red hand knitted beanie and scarf from her grandmother, and a box game called 'Monopoly' from her aunt and uncle.

At her request, Rachel's mother, aunt and grandmother move back to the dining table, and commence to play 'Monopoly'. Her uncle declines, saying, "I think I've had enough buying and selling for the day Rachel, if you don't mind," and promptly heads off to his bedroom to change into his golf clothes. A little while later he passes by to peck them all on the cheek and heads off in anticipation of an afternoon's golf, leaving 'the girls", he said, "to battle it out between themselves."

"Living in town has its advantages," her mother says quietly, as she passes play-money over to Rachel, the banker, and Rachel hands her the property card she has just bought.

"Yes," Dawn says, matter-of-factly. "I couldn't live on a farm anymore now."

Rachel looks up suddenly towards her grandmother, after her aunt's words. She notices her grandmother hasn't even seemed to notice the comment, but after a few minutes, she says, "Yes, you never liked the farm, especially after you went away to Springwood. It was a good thing you married Joe; a 'towney', as we used to call them when I was younger." She winks at Rachel, who relaxes again.

"Well, at least two of us stayed on the land Mum," Betty mumbles, watching Dawn's monopoly piece being sent to 'Jail', after being instructed to move her monopoly piece there by a 'Chance' card.

"Yes, dear," she says, as she looks at Betty and smiles. "It's nice knowing Neville is still working the old place too, with the boys…"

That reminds me," Aunt Dawn interrupts. "The boys called in to see us on their way to a concert or something in Sydney, a few weeks ago, Rachel. I told them we would be seeing you soon. They both asked me to wish you a happy birthday from them, and Matty said something about it being time his only cousin became a lady. He wanted me to tell you that. He said you'd know what he meant." Her aunt waits expectantly for Rachel's response.

Rachel rolls her eyes. "He's such a stirrer. He keeps reminding me about the time I was at their place and I was running and slipped over in the mud. I was covered in it, so I had to change into some of Luke's clothes after that until I got home," Rachel replies, but thinks, *what's wrong with being a tomboy anyway, Darel doesn't seem to care?*

"Well, you're thirteen now, and a young lady, that's for sure," Nana chips in, and Rachel grins at her. *My number one supporter,* she thinks, although she is surprised her mother hasn't made a comment, one way or the other. But then she notices her mother doesn't look like she's been listening.

It's your turn Betty," Aunt Dawn says, shaking Betty from her thoughts.

The afternoon visit draws to a close. Betty announces that it's time to go. Rachel's grandmother asks her to wait for a moment. She then asks Rachel to follow her and they walk to a room at the end of the hallway. The room is full of her grandmother's belongings, including all her books.

"I know I've already given you that hat and scarf for your birthday, but there's something else I want you to have" she says, as she stops in front of her bookcase and begins to scan the shelves.

Rachel waits patiently while her grandmother taps her fingers along the books lined up in front of her. "Ah, here it is." She pulls out a book with a ragged paper cover and hands it to her. "This is a story about a girl who loves her home too," she says. "I think you might find it interesting, but it doesn't matter if you decide not to read it until you're older," she says thoughtfully. "Either way, I want you to have it *now*."

Rachel takes the book and is about to look at the cover when her mother calls from the front door. "Rachel, we really must go. We don't want to be late getting you back to Trinity."

Her grandmother promptly spins Rachel around and gently pushes her towards the door. Rachel turns and gives her grandmother a big cuddle. "Thank you Nana. I love you."

"I love you too Rachel," her grandmother replies.

They walk to the front door, where her mother and aunt wait.

It isn't until both Rachel and her mother pull their arms inside the car, after enthusiastically waving goodbye to the two ladies standing at the front of the house, that Rachel looks down at the book in her lap. The title on the cover, 'Gone With The Wind', stares up at her. She opens it and reads a little of the first chapter, discovering that it is a story set in America, and that the girl, named Scarlett, lives on a plantation, which she imagines would probably be like a property or big farm, in Australia. She closes it and lifts it to her nose, and sniffs. *I love the smell of old books. It always reminds me of Nana.*

Thinking about how she loves the *smell* of old books, reminds her of how Darel had once said he loved the *shape* of books. He had said that when she had given him a book for his birthday one year. She had looked at him with a queer look on her face when he had said it, and he had laughed, and explained. "Well Rach, I love the shape of books because it's a dead give-away before I open the present. It's fun trying to figure out what book you'll be giving me next though."

They are almost half way to Trinity when Rachel realises both she and her mother have hardly spoken to each other, lost in their own thoughts.

"I had a good time Mum, thank you," she says.

Betty reaches across and pats her on her leg. "I'm glad Rachel," taking her eyes briefly from the road to cast a quick smile her way.

"Mum, how come Aunty Dawn didn't have any kids?" she asks.

Betty balks a little, wondering how to explain it to a thirteen year old, and then decides to go the easy path. "Well, it just didn't happen, Rachel."

"But, didn't she *want* kids?" Rachel presses.

"Yes, she did, she loves children. She was a teacher once, remember, just like I was?" She knows she'd better come up with something more though, to pacify Rachel's curious mind. "Some people just don't seem to be able to have children the way others do Rachel. I had hoped for a brother or sister for you too. It would have been nice for you to have had a sister like I did." *And a brother, for your father,* she thinks. "But at least you have your two cousins at Dubbo, even if they are boys and older than you. Well, that's one reason why you're at Trinity now. So you can be around other girl's your age," she concludes.

Rachel nods her head to show her mother she has heard. *Trust her to bring it back around to Trinity,* she stews, while Betty decides she must try to find an appropriate book on the subject of reproduction for her. She knows Rachel has seen enough of it with the livestock on the farm, but somehow she doesn't think she's going to get away with leaving it all up to her to piece together, like her mother did to her.

Betty thinks about her sister and brother-in-law when she is on her way home to Binda, after dropping Rachel back at Trinity.

Rachel's questioning, on top of her sister's and mother's remarks today about living in town, have made her think about when she was younger.

She remembers how she had felt sorry for her sister, at first, for not being able to have children. But that sentiment had progressively passed, as Joe's business improved, they bought the new house they now live in, and often travelled abroad for holidays. She still had all the postcards from her sister's trips overseas stacked away in a bottom cupboard somewhere. Of course, the overseas trips had stopped after her father passed away, and her mother went to live with them.

She has always been a little envious of her elder sister, even though she's close to her. They had been play mates growing up, like her brother's sons had also been on her parent's farm. They had helped one another learn about life, shared confidences and experiences. Anyone would immediately assume that sending Rachel to Trinity had been for reasons such as these, or the lack thereof. That may well have been the case, even if Darel hadn't entered the picture. In a way, she should be grateful he had, she supposes, because it had spurred her on to do what was necessary.

There had not only been changes for Rachel over the last year, but for her too. She was no longer president of the Parent's and Citizen's Association at Barwon, now Rachel was no longer at school there. She was still secretary for the Red Cross and the Country Women's Association though, so that kept her reasonably busy with meetings and fundraising.

But she was still surprised by how much extra time she now had with Rachel being at Trinity. It was hard *not* to notice her absence. She misses her, although she won't ever tell Rachel and give her another excuse to ask to leave. That would be just asking for more grief.

It's a good thing her sister lives in town, for her mother's sake, she reflects; closer to medical services and to keep her entertained with outings to the various parks and coffee shops Dawn said they visit on shopping days. She said their mother was good company for her too, because although it wasn't the same as working on the land, Joe still worked long hours, which often included the weekends.

Betty wonders what it would be like, living in town. She had lived in a town when she had been at boarding school and Teacher's College, but that had been a long time ago. It would be different now, at her stage of life, although she had known of others who had made the change well.

Bill's father, George, was one. He moved to Dubbo a few years after his wife, Alice, died. He retired from farming, leaving Binda to Bill. The original homestead nestled atop a hill overlooking the newer home that Bill and Betty had moved into had been emptied and locked up ever since. Betty had cleaned and washed for him after Alice died. She had even prepared most of his meals, or invited him to eat with them. But, one day he just announced that he'd had enough, that he had to move on. He said he missed Alice too much, and there were too many memories on the farm.

They had both wondered how he would cope with the change as they helped him move. He had grown up and worked all his life on the land. But he seemed to take to it like a duck to water, living in town in his retirement home, having a yarn with his neighbours when he felt like a bit of company, or playing lawn bowls at the club.

She tries to imagine herself, living in a more modern house in Dubbo. The farm house at Binda may have been newly built for her and Bill eighteen years ago, but it would be nice to have a more modern home, and especially a newer kitchen with all the latest gadgets, like her sister has. It would also be a lot easier to be close to everything without having to travel long distances too. Perhaps one day, after Bill passes.

All of a sudden she admonishes herself. *What am I thinking?* I married a farmer. We'll both be at Binda for a good while yet. Perhaps I had better get stuck into some more gardening; the white rose hedge surrounding the house is in need of serious pruning. *Heaven forbid if anything should ever happen to Bill.*

CHAPTER 7

The small white bus pulls up at the gateway to the property and Mr Weber ushers Rachel and her five companions out the door, following behind. He motions for the girls to collect their backpacks as he commences removing them from the luggage compartment at the side of the bus.

"Now girls, there's your starting point." He points to the other side of the gateway. "I have your checklist of everything you've packed, so you're right to go. Are there any questions?" their assessor asks, looking at each face individually.

Mandy Morris looks around at the open bushland over the fence with a worried look. "What happens if we get lost," she mutters.

"Well that's part of this exercise, if you'll remember Mandy; to test your navigational skills," Mr Weber answers. "So far, you've each completed the requirements up to this point for the Bronze level, Duke of Edinburgh award, which includes the training for this section. This overnight hiking trip is the final activity."

"So, how come we don't *all* have maps?" Mandy retorts,

pouting.

Rachel rolls her eyes and notices Jess attempting to conceal a smirk.

"Mandy Morris, you would do well to remember the importance of team work, especially at this level of your award," Mr Weber says with obvious annoyance.

He looks at Rachel. "Rachel, perhaps Mandy could do with some additional navigational practice. Give her the map please."

"But Mr Weber," Rachel reacts with disgust, "we *will* get lost if I give her the map."

Jess, standing beside Rachel, throws her hand across her mouth and turns her head to the side, to stifle an outburst of laughter.

"Rachel, do as I say," Mr Weber responds firmly, ignoring Jess's semi-outburst.

Rachel thrusts the map into Mandy's hands.

"Thank you Rachel." Mr Weber looks at her deadpanned, and she's immediately reminded that he is not only their assessor for the Duke of Edinburgh Award, but also her biased history teacher. *He's never liked me since I asked that question in class.*

"Now, follow your itinerary and remember, the Rutledge family have kindly allowed you access to part of their property, as well as their shearing shed to sleep in tonight.

Make sure you leave everything as you find it and put out all fires, completely. I'll be waiting for you at the low-level bridge at Oakley tomorrow afternoon, at two. Are you all clear on that?"

He scans the faces of the girls in front of him. When they all nod, he brightens. "Off you go then."

He walks over and unlatches the gate, watches them pick up their backpacks and walk to the other side. He closes the gate and returns to the bus.

After the bus departs, Jess and Deb wait for Rachel, watching her pull out a compass from one of the compartments of her backpack and push it into the pocket of her jeans.

Mandy has already headed off with her side-kick Chloe and her newest follower, Melanie Gray, walking in single file behind her.

"Well, so far, everything's looking normal," Jess says to Rachel as they start walking. "So much for team-work."

"Yeah, I know. But at least with the three of them in front, we can keep an eye on them," Rachel responds.

"Hey, who packed the sausages for tea tonight," Deb asks as she catches up after stopping briefly to remove a thistle stuck to the leg of her jeans.

"Mandy. She insisted. Said she wanted to make sure she wasn't going to starve," Jess answers, giggling.

"Well, I hope she's keeping them cool. It's going to be a hot day," Rachel says, looking up at the sun.

Rachel was *glad* she'd chosen to join the Duke of Edinburgh Award program; *another tick to 'Pollyanna'*, she thinks. *I guess there was a reason Mum made me read that book.*

When she had read the brochure about the Duke of Edinburgh Award program she had been given, on the way home to Binda at the end of second form, she had been instantly interested. It wasn't the awards offered that stirred her interest, it was the list of activities that she would need to do.

She was already a member of the netball team and played the piano, so they could be included in the physical recreation and skill sections. Then there was volunteer work, which had ended up consisting of visiting an elderly person one afternoon every week for an hour or two. She had found it very enjoyable and wondered why it was called, *work*. To her it was almost like visiting her Nana in Bathurst, or her Grandad in Dubbo, and she found the stories the elderly people told her, fascinating.

But, the best part of the program for Rachel was the section on expedition. She couldn't imagine why she would need to be rewarded for going on long walks through the bush and sleeping under the stars, or even in a shearing shed, like tonight. She was looking forward to the Silver level more though, when they would be sleeping outside.

She didn't care about the Bronze, Silver and Gold award certificates or medals she would receive when all the boxes had been ticked. She would put in the time and effort required, purely for the enjoyment of it. It may not be the same as being at Binda all the time, but it was the closest she was ever going to get to it. And it was nice having Jess and Deb's company for the expeditions.

The first three, of the six, fourteen-year-old girls, walking in single file, made noisy progress across the grass lands and through the bush that Mandy led them through.

Rachel thought it probably wasn't a bad thing, because the noise would keep any snakes away, and it allowed her to look around more, instead of solely where her feet were going. She still needed to pay attention to her feet though because she had never seen so many scattered rocks and pebbles in the same area before. Other than for the abundance of rocks, the vegetation was fairly similar to Binda, spear and kangaroo grass underfoot, occasional patterns of Patterson's curse and a variety of eucalypt shrubs and trees.

When they'd reached the more wooded area she had looked up at startled honeyeaters and tree sparrows. She hadn't seen or heard a kookaburra laugh yet, but it was still early. She thought of Darel; she always did whenever she saw or heard a kookaburra.

They had been walking steadily for close to an hour and a half, when they reached a stream.

"Well, so far, so good, our first landmark," Deb says, catching up to the others from the rear of the line.

"Yeah, but can we cross it here?" Jess says, edging to look closer at the fast moving stream of water bubbling over several large boulders.

Rachel looks over to Mandy and holds out her hand, "Let me look at the map please."

"No, this is where we marked to cross over, and this is where we'll cross over," she snarls back, clutching the map firmly.

Ignoring Mandy, Rachel looks downstream and then upstream, and turns back to them all. "It's probably a bit shallower down there," she points, "around the bend."

"I didn't think you tough country people would be afraid of a bit of water?" Mandy sneers.

"Mandy, grow up," Rachel retorts. "I just don't want anyone to slip on the rocks and get hurt."

"We'll be right, just follow me." Mandy proceeds to step quickly across the first and second closest boulders, and as she turns to gloat about how easy it is, to those behind her, her front foot gives way from under her and she falls backwards into the water.

The map falls from her hand, quickly sinking out of sight beneath the water, and Rachel groans. Meanwhile, Mandy manages to pull herself up to a sitting position despite the heavy backpack weighing her down, bends forward, turns and crawls her way back over the boulders to where the five other girls stand, watching her.

"You were saying..." Jess is the first to speak.

"Ok, so I slipped. *Big Deal*! If Rachel hadn't opened her mouth, it probably wouldn't have happened."

Rachel has had enough. "Oh for...Mandy, just put a sock in it, will ya, for *once*? We're all in this together, so can you at least *try* to get on with me?"

Rachel walks over to Mandy, sitting on the ground, and begins to help her remove her backpack. "You'd better check to see if everything in your backpack is alright," she says with a big sigh.

Mandy is momentarily stumped by Rachel's offer of assistance, and allows her guard to come down. "What are we gunna do now the maps gone?" She looks up at Rachel sheepishly now, remembering how it slipped out of her hand and disappeared.

"I have the compass, and I know which direction the shearing shed is from here, so that's a start," Rachel reassures her. "Are you ok?" she adds, hoping she is. Although Mandy often drove her mad with her incessant digs and moaning, ever since she's had that talk with her grandmother, she's tried hard to ignore it. In any event, she doesn't want to see her injured.

"Yeah, I guess," Mandy replies, looking dejectedly at her wet clothes.

Rachel turns and walks over to sit beside Jess on a grassy patch, while Mandy checks her backpack and finally announces that everything inside has remained dry, except a light weight raincoat she had placed nearest to the outside. They all laugh at the irony of it, which lightens the mood.

Mandy changes into a skimpy top and shorts, wrapping her wet jeans and shirt around the outside of her backpack.

Rachel considers suggesting it would have been better to leave her jeans and shirt on, but decides against it. Now that they were all getting on better together, she doesn't want to risk setting Mandy off again. Besides, the wet clothes should keep the sausages a bit cooler in her back pack. The summer sun beats down on their hat-covered heads as they head off, but this time, with Rachel in the lead.

A few hours later, they reach the shearing shed, much to the relief of all. Mandy has complained of scratches and bites all over her legs for the last hour and there is little doubt she'll be silent when she has to pull her backpack over her reddened sunburnt shoulders tomorrow morning.

They find the rain-water tank at the side of the shed and

replenish their water supplies. Then they investigate the shed. They deposit their backpacks on to the floor and prepare their sleeping bags for the night.

Jess and Debbie arrange theirs either side of Rachel's in the centre of the building. Mandy, Chloe and Melanie decide to line theirs up with their heads alongside the wall in the furthermost corner.

Rachel thinks about the shearing sheds at Binda and Jannali. The one they are sleeping in tonight is fairly similar to the one at Binda, a newer timber construction with corrugated galvanised iron cladding and roof. But the one at Jannali was entirely different. It has sandstone walls and smooth uneven floor boards. She remembers asking her father why they were different, having explored all the outer sheds and buildings at both properties with Darel when they were in primary school.

Her father told her that all the buildings at Jannali had been built more than a hundred years before the buildings at Binda, and in those days they had had to use the building materials that were available close by.

She had tried to listen attentively when he went on to explain what all the buildings on Binda were made from, although her interest had started to fade. That was, until he began to tell her about the buildings at Jannali and in particular, the original homestead and people who once lived there. At that point she had hung on to every word.

"The Jannali house," he said, "was the first house built in the Dubbo area, by Darel's, great-great grandfather. It's what's called, a slab-hut, made from timber, bark, mud, clay and all sorts of natural materials." He had paused then, looking at her intently, before continuing.

"Darel's father told me that Darel's great-great grandfather was friendly with the aborigines who had lived in the area before the other settlers came. He learned a lot from them about the Australian bush and the best natural materials to use to help him build the Jannali slab-hut."

"But, Darel's home isn't a *hut* Dad, it's *huge*! When I first went there I nearly got lost inside, there were so many different rooms," she had admonished him with a frown.

Her father had laughed at her indignation. "Yes, it's a *proper* home, no doubt about that. Old man Rutherford was a wealthy man, Rachel. He owned a great deal more property back then too. He even owned Binda!" he had replied, wide eyed, waiting for her eyes to light up with surprise. He was not let down. But, her mother had come into the lounge room from the kitchen at that moment, and looked at her father with a look that Rachel thought had always been saved for her, when she had done something wrong. So, their conversation had come to an end.

Over the next few hours, the girls collect kindling, some

larger, broken branches and rocks from the bush to prepare a fire site. Finally, they organise their supplies.

As evening descends, they light the fire and once it has died down to hot coals, Mandy brings a plate of squashed sausages to the fire and Deb cooks them, while Chloe hands around bent and broken slices of bread. They somehow manage not to make jokes about the state of the sausages and bread which had both been in Mandy's backpack.

While they are eating their sausage sandwiches heartily, talking and jumping in fright at sounds emanating from the bush close around them, John Pritchard pulls up in his utility, behind a concealed tree lined section of the hill overlooking the shearing shed. He watches the girls for a few moments and returns to his home to ring Mr Weber and reassure him that all looks well for his six students. He hadn't been asked to check up on the girls, and Mr Weber had made it clear that they were to be self-sufficient, but it had only taken him about a ten minute drive from the farm house to make sure they were alright.

After their sausage sandwich meal and a general clean-up, the girls languish around the fire toasting marshmallows, gazing into the fire and talking, until the red embers turn black and there is no longer any sign of smoke. They make their way to the lighted shed and race each other to their sleeping bags. No-one wants to have to turn off the light and find their way in the dark, although several of them have torches in their backpacks.

Rachel closes her eyes and listens to the noises outside. An owl is hooting in the distance and she hears a possum scurrying across the roof of the shed. She is soothed by the nocturnal noises and although she's tired, she fights to stay awake a little longer, just so she can listen to them.

Chloe is whispering to Mandy and they wriggle in their sleeping bags, no doubt, closer together. Melanie must be asleep already. Jess and Debbie are both breathing heavily too, so she mustn't be the only one she surmises. She decides she should join them. They have to find the low-level bridge at Oakley tomorrow, without a map. She drifts off, attempting to stamp to her memory, the landmarks she recalls seeing along the route they had planned on the map.

"Ahhh, get it off, get it off."

Rachel reaches for her torch and quickly turns the beam to the location of the noise.

Chloe is struggling to stand up in her sleeping bag and flicking her hands repeatedly through her hair. She topples over on to Mandy and Melanie, and they all start yelling and shrieking.

Jess and Deb get out of their sleeping bags and race to turn on the shed light, unaware of each other in the darkness. They both reach the light switch at the same time and fumble to turn it on with each other's fingers in the way.

Finally, the bright light floods the shed, and the six girls squint and blink rapidly, as they try to quickly accustom their eyes from the previous darkness.

"Get off me," Mandy bellows at Chloe who is still struggling to find her balance on top of her.

Melanie has rolled to the side and is now finally stepping out of her sleeping bag.

Rachel turns off her torch, steps out of her sleeping bag and walks over to help Chloe. Chloe looks pleadingly at Rachel while running her hands over her hair repeatedly. "Is there anything still there Rachel," she whimpers. Rachel checks her hair, and Chloe turns around so she can look at her back too.

All of a sudden Mandy exclaims, "There it is," and points to a large grey spider scurrying off to the side and disappearing between the wall and floor.

"Ohhh, yuk," Melanie exclaims. I won't be able to sleep now.

Rachel doesn't like spiders herself, but she knows that no one will get any sleep unless someone pulls it together.

"Why don't we all sleep in the middle of the room, away from the walls," she suggests, *and away from where spiders lurk.*

Although there was no one in the area to notice, that night the shearing shed light was left on, and by morning, six sleeping bags filled with bodies, lay bunched together in the middle of the floor.

At day break they were all woken by a mixture of bird calls outside. Rachel smiles at the sound of the kookaburras amidst the din, and races outside. She gasps with delight when she sees a family of kangaroos grazing nearby, and a baby kangaroo in the pouch of one of them. As she steps through the door though, she startles them, and they bound away into the bush.

Even though it is early summer, there is still a chill in the air from the temperature dropping through the night, so she decides to relight the fire. As she's collecting some kindling nearby, she thinks about Darel's dreaming story about how the kangaroo got her pouch, and his narration of it:

'This story is about a mother kangaroo, her baby Joey and an old wombat. When the world was young, the mother kangaroo didn't have a pouch like she has now. Not having a pouch made it hard for her to look after Joey, because as soon as her back was turned her baby would wander off exploring.

One day an old and grumpy wombat turned up. He kept complaining, over and over, about being weary and blind, and not having a friend in the world. When he told the mother kangaroo that he hadn't had anything to drink or eat for days, she felt sorry for him, even though he wouldn't stop grumbling. She told him she would be his friend and help him. She told him to hold onto her tail and she would take him to water and food.

So off they went, although it took a long time to get to where she wanted to take him, because the old wombat had trouble holding onto her tail. She had been very patient. But, by the time the old wombat was drinking and eating, she realised she needed to get back to Joey.

So, she took off, and after searching high and low, she finally found Joey asleep under an old gum tree. She figured he was alright, so she bounded back to where she had left the old wombat to make sure he was still alright too.

The mother kangaroo was almost back to where she had left the old wombat when she sensed danger. Then she spotted a hunter moving close to the old wombat, so she made a lot of noise to distract him and led him far away, until the hunter finally gave up and went home.

By now, she was worrying again about Joey, so she bounded back to where she had last seen him, and with great relief found him still asleep under the old gum tree. She woke him and together they made their way slowly back to where she had left the old wombat. But no matter how much they searched they couldn't find him.

The reason they couldn't find the old wombat is because he had in fact been, Biyaami, the Creator Spirit, who had come down from the sky to test the kindness of his creatures.

The mother kangaroo was rewarded for her kindness. Biyaami presented her with a dilly-bag to tie around her waist, so she could carry Joey wherever she went. When she tied it to her waist though, the dilly bag magically turned it into a pouch. And, from then on, Joey could be kept safe. She didn't need to worry about him getting lost again because she could take him with her wherever she went.'

Rachel likes the way the dreaming stories always seem to have a moral of some type. They teach and reward kindness, respect and responsibility when it is shown, not only to other people but to the environment as well. She imagines aborigine mothers telling the dreaming stories to their young children as they go about their daily lives, after seeing a family of kangaroos just like she had.

The fire is burning well now. She heads around to the tank for a morning wash, returning only a few minutes later to see Mandy and Chloe cooking some sausages.

"I thought we cooked all those last night."

"No, I left some for this morning, for breakfast." Mandy smiles, looking very pleased with her foresightedness.

"Are you sure they're alright though," Rachel asks with a frown.

"Yeah, why wouldn't they be? It was cool last night. They smell ok," she says taking a good sniff at the pan. "Want one," she asks Rachel.

"No thanks. I think I'll stick to an orange."

"Suit yourself," Mandy replies, "More for us."

An hour later they are on their way, heading north. By the time they reach the dirt road as expected, they notice Mandy and Chloe have fallen some distance behind, so they decide to stop for a break. By the time they catch up though, they are both holding their stomachs and groaning. Next minute they drop their backpacks and take off running behind a group of trees nearby.

"Oh, *nooo*!" Debbie looks in the direction the two girls went. "They were the only ones who ate the sausages this morning."

When Mandy and Chloe finally come out from behind the trees, they stagger towards the rest of the group and collapse under the shade of a big gum tree nearby.

"I can't go any further," Mandy moans.

"Me either," Chloe adds, and then crawls a little distance away and retches.

"We have to get help," Jess says, watching Mandy and Chloe with concern.

"Yeah, we do," Rachel agrees, and moves into action. "Ok, we can't leave them alone. Someone has to stay."

"I'll stay," Melanie says, without hesitation, and immediately walks over and collects Mandy and Chloe's back packs from where they had dropped them before running for the bushes. She takes them over to the sick girls, rummages through each backpack, and pulls out their water bottles. She then assists the two girls to lay their heads back against them.

Rachel, Jess and Deb watch as Melanie tends to Mandy and Chloe. Rachel's glad that Melanie is part of their Duke of

Edinburgh group. The unwell girls are lucky to have her for a friend too, she decides.

Deb moves closer to Rachel and Jess. "I think I'd better stay too. I don't think we should leave Melanie by herself with these two the way they are."

Rachel nods. "Ok then, I think Jess and I should head for Oakley, or the direction I think it's in..." She looks down at her compass. "Yeah, because there's no point doubling back to try to find the Rutlidge's house. We don't know how far away it is from the shearing shed. I think finding Mr Weber will be quicker..."

Jess continues, "...but, if we see a farm house on the way, we'll go straight there...agreed? She looks at Rachel.

"Yep, agreed," Rachel says, and Deb nods. "Ok."

Rachel and Jess take off as fast as they can, following landmarks that come to Rachel's memory as they walk. Rachel checks her compass periodically. The thought of the other's in their group waiting for help spurs them on as they walk briskly up each hill they climb and scour the countryside for any sign of habitation.

"I guess that's why we were told to choose this area. It's a test and a half, being so far away from civilisation." Rachel says to Jess, grimacing.

Rachel was just about to start questioning her memory and her compass skills, when they pull themselves over yet, another hill, and discover the river, sparkling below, on the other side of a road. They both immediately scamper down the hill and on to the road, looking right and left, for any signs of the low level bridge. They spot it to their right, about half a kilometre away and are just about to start running when a white bus comes hurtling around the corner and pulls up abruptly beside them.

Once Mr Weber hears their story, and Rachel tells him the girl's location, it is only a matter of minutes before Mandy and Cloe are collected and then dropped off at the hospital. Two days later, they are fully recovered from their food poisoning episode.

The six girls receive their Bronze awards, despite Mandy, Chloe, Melanie and Deb not completing the hike to the designated end point. Mr Weber tells them, that given the circumstances, they had all worked well together as a team, exercising clear judgment and implementing an excellent rescue procedure.

It also became surprisingly clear to Rachel that the experience had altered Mandy's attitude towards her.

When she approached Rachel, after arriving back at Trinity from hospital, she thanked her for 'saving her', Rachel hadn't needed to wonder if Mandy were setting her up, just to get her guard down before striking again, as had often been the case. This time, she had sensed the sincerity behind her words and noticed the humble look in her eyes. *I guess they don't look out for one another in the city, like we do in the country,* she decides.

CHAPTER 8

By the time Rachel and Darel were both fifteen, they knew a great deal about each other's High School experiences. Every school holidays they caught up on what had happened during the previous term, although during Form One, that hadn't been the case.

During that first year, Rachel had intentionally not talked about Trinity. It hadn't taken Darel long to realise by her abrupt answers and sullen expressions to questions he asked about Trinity, that the less he broached the subject, the happier she was during the holidays. So, although he was curious about everything about her life at boarding school, he had no intention of pursuing it, until she was ready.

It had seemed to Rachel, that Darel hadn't wanted to discuss anything about Dubbo High either, when he had remained quieter than usual that first year. At first, she had wondered if she had offended him, by not wanting to talk about Trinity, because when she had tried to find out about Dubbo High, she had received the same short responses she had given, in return. But, it wasn't like Darel to – pay back, so she decided to think no more about it. After all, she had been absorbed in her own private dilemma, anyway, during that time.

They had both seemed happy enough to leave the topic of school absent from their time together during the holidays. That was, until their second year when, as if by mutual consent, the subject suddenly became available for discussion. They then had a year's worth of information to catch up on, beginning with Darel answering Rachel's questions at length.

He told her about his school and teachers and how some of the kids they both went to primary school with were now also going to Dubbo High. "But I still don't hang out with them Rach," he said. "It doesn't bother me one bit though, 'cause I've made some other friends from Dubbo."

He was a member of the school football and cricket teams, and played a fair bit of tennis too. His mother often drove him to inter-school competitions around the district. She could tell he was pretty good at cricket and tennis because as the years unfolded, he'd tell her about his latest batting average or bowling victory with a proud look on his face. He also told her how he'd been nicknamed 'Ace" because he'd worked hard on his serve, and often won tennis matches that way.

Sometimes, his mate, Pete, who lived on a property nearer to Dubbo, would stay for the weekend with him, or he would stay with Pete. They would ride their father's motor bikes around the farms and camp out beneath the stars at night. "He doesn't live by the river like we do though Rach" he said.

When he first told her about Pete, her smiled response hadn't looked convincing, and he had somehow known what she had been feeling. He had looked at her thoughtfully and said, "You'll always be my best friend though Rach, no matter what."

Rachel had wondered at that time if she would ever have the opportunity to go camping with Darel, like Pete did. She knew her mother wouldn't let her camp out by the river with him, even though she couldn't think of anything better; sleeping under the stars and watching the moonlight sparkle on the water with him by her side. It was an image she found difficult to cast aside, and would often drift off to sleep at Trinity thinking about it.

So, although it wasn't *exactly* what she had hoped for, the expedition for the Silver award, Duke of Edinburgh, to the Warrumbungle National Park had come close to it, and she was bursting at the seams to tell Darel all about it in their mid-year holidays.

"To think, the Park is actually not all that far from here Darel, about an hour and a half drive, in that direction," she points to the north, confidently. "We even drove through

Dubbo to get there, although we had to take the highway and bypass Barwon. When we first arrived at the Park, we were taken to the information centre where we learned all about the Warrumbungles. They had information to read all around the centre, but when I came to the part about the history of the area, guess what?" and without waiting for a reply, she continued, "I read that 'Warrumbungle' means 'crooked mountain'; an aboriginal word used by a different tribe to your mother's. I can't remember which tribe now though," she says, biting her bottom lip in concentration, but quickly gives up and continues with gusto, "but, it was a spiritual place for several different tribes, *including* the Wiradjuri," she told Darel, feeling proud of being able to tell him something pertaining to his mother. "And when I started reading more about the history of the area, you'll never guess," she said, barely able to contain her excitement now. "It was there, in black and white, about your great-great grandfather, Samuel Rutherford, and how he had the first squatter runs along the Macquarie River. Yes," she nods vigorously, as she watches Darel's eyes open wide with interest. "And later we went to the Siding Springs Observatory. That was where we were able to look at the stars through a huge telescope, even though it was day time. And Venus, wow, Venus looks so amazing up close. I wish you could see it all Darel," she had said, finally finishing her verbal tirade with a big sigh.

Darel had been enthralled by her narration. She hadn't looked this happy for a long time he thought as he watched her eyes sparkle and the words tumble from her mouth. She looked even more beautiful, if that were possible, when she was excited, he noted. But, when she bit her bottom lip, well, he had had to concentrate on what she was saying really hard; she had the most perfect pink lips. He had wondered why he had never noticed that before.

"Maybe we could go there together one day Rach. Camp out," he had said.

Rachel had held her breath when he had said that, to gain control of her words, so she wouldn't blurt out that that was all she had been thinking about since the expedition. She managed to reply, calmly, "Yes, that would be so cool," with a smile.

For some reason, she feels a bit tongue-tied now he has mentioned camping together, so she covers it up by prattling on…"We saw the most amazing things. Of course, there were kangaroos, wallabies, koalas and we got pestered by the flies and ants," she grimaces, remembering how Jess had nearly eaten a fly in her baked beans, how Mandy had swallowed one when it flew in her mouth, and how Melanie had sat on an ant's nest and they had all slapped her repeatedly to get them off. "There were some really beautiful turquoise parrots, and a wedge-tailed eagle there too. But the view at the summit of Mount Exmouth; well, it just takes your breath away Darel. When you look out from it you can see the whole park; all the sharp ridges and green valleys below, and even to the edge of the Great Dividing Range to the east, and the plains that seem to go on forever to the west. A photo could never do it justice." She closes her eyes and she can hear the tree tops swaying in the breeze, and smell the water that is gently flowing past from the river. "It's almost like Binda; you have to be there, to understand." She opens her eyes to see Darel watching her intently.

"Well, let's make a promise, to go there together one day Rach. I know you're good for it."

"I keep my promises," she says cheekily, remembering telling him that when she was about six years old.

"I know," he says with a wide grin, and she knows he is thinking about the very same memory.

Later that night, Rachel is lying on her bed and finishes updating her diary. She notices that about a quarter of the book is still blank. She had chosen the biggest diary available when she had bought it. It was a five-year one, but she had decided that if she crossed out the date at the top of each page, it should last for the entire time she was at Trinity. Although she was expected to be at Trinity for six years she had still held on to the hope that she would be permitted to leave before then, so she would have more than enough pages to write in, either way. Besides, she didn't write in it every day, and as she flips back to the first few entries she notices that she hadn't written anything for about six months from the beginning of Second Form. That had been because Mandy had read the previous entries, she remembers.

Once she had returned to the dormitory that day with Jess, she had locked her diary with the little golden key that she'd found in the bottom of her beauty case. She kept the key in her hand and the diary close by, until everyone went to tea. She had then quickly hidden the diary at the back of her clothes cubicle. She placed the key, attached to a long piece of ribbon she also found in her beauty case, around her neck. From then on she had never taken it off, except to hang it up near her towel in the shower cubicle. Never again was she ever going to give anyone the opportunity to read her most private thoughts, or Darel's stories.

She flips back to some earlier entries and can't help but notice how desperately sad she had sounded at the beginning. She had poured out her heart at her loneliness and how much she missed Binda and Darel. She wonders why Mandy had chosen to tease her about Darel's stories, instead of making fun of her for being a sook. Knowing Mandy as well as she did, she's sure she would have targeted Rachel's weakest spot. Perhaps she had shown a smidgen of kindness by not mentioning her vulnerability at the time. Or perhaps she had also been feeling a lot the same and didn't want to draw attention to it. Having said that, maybe she had just found Darel's stories much more interesting. In any event, she had never mentioned anything in her diary to anyone else. Well, as far as she knew anyway.

Scanning the pages of her diary, she notices that although she's written about Darel and the things they did during the school holidays, she hasn't entered any more dreaming stories after her second year of high school. She had written them from memory too, so although she had re-read them many times, he had never told her any new stories since primary school. Maybe his mother has already told him all the dreaming stories and Wiradjuri words she knows. She decides to ask him about it the next day, in case he has any more she doesn't know about.

***

"Yeah, well, she *has* told me all the stories and words that she remembers," he says, looking a bit guarded.

Rachel would have accepted that and not asked any more about it, if he hadn't looked like he was hiding something.

"If you don't want to tell me about them anymore Darel, it's ok," she says with downcast eyes.

"Seriously Rach, it's true," he says looking at her with a grimace, still feeling a little guilty. He looks closely at his best friend's face, and notices her lips turning down at the corners. He doesn't want to have any secrets from her, but...well, she caught him off guard. He's kept this one to himself for quite a while now. If she hadn't mentioned the stories he might have been able to keep it that way.

He had been pretty cut up about it when he had found out. It was a good thing it had happened when she was away at the time. Even when she had come home for the first few holidays he had still been trying to wrap his head around it. It had been a huge relief when she hadn't wanted to talk about school. It had made it easier not to tell her, and besides, she had been going through a fair bit herself in that first year. What he had found out; well, it had changed the way he looked at a lot of things afterwards.

Should he tell her, even now, knowing her; knowing how much she hates injustice, how upset she gets about it? But then again, he shouldn't sell her short either. She can be a lot tougher than she looks. Plus, she's older now. Besides, she's knows I'm keeping something from her and she'll give me grief until I tell her. She'll be mad as hell when she finds out I kept it from her for three years too. Maybe being mad will help. That thought makes up his mind for him...

"But, I found out about something else about Mum, because of some things that happened at school in First Form"

Rachel looks up suddenly. "In *First Form*! What happened

at school in First Form?" she asks, looking put out.

He decides to ease into it. "Well, a lot of aborigines go to Dubbo High too; the ones from Dubbo. I don't know any of them very well, because I spend most of my time with Pete. They mostly hang out together. They don't' seem to want to get to know anyone else. You know me though, I treat everyone the same." He pauses, thinking, "There was this one bloke though, who played cricket with me back then. We got on ok, or so I thought, anyway. One day I asked him if he knew of any shops in town that sold aborigine art and stuff. I was thinking of having a look for Mum for a birthday present. You know how she likes to paint and make things?"

Rachel's eyes light up. "Yeah, like the butterfly doll you gave me for my birthday when I was little? Hmm, what's it called again?"

"Buuja-Buuja," Darel answers. "But it means butterfly, so you were right in a way," he says smiling. "You still got it?"

"Yeah, of course. Your Mum made her for me, hand painted her with all those bright coloured patterns. She's always been special to me." She can see that Darel has perked up a bit by her comments, although she has a feeling it's not going to last long. "Anyway, you were telling me about the boy you played cricket with..."

"Yeah, well after I asked him about it, you know, about a

shop, he looked at me real strange, and said, 'Whatcha wanna know about black fella stuff for anyway, being a gabaa 'n all.' I mean, it's not like he hadn't seen my Mum, so I didn't think he'd react that way. Anyway, he avoided me after that." He considers how Rachel has taken things. So far, so good. He continues, "I guess he thought I was having a go at him...go figure. Anyway, it didn't bother me that much. I sort of understood, but — it was the way Mum was treated that got my back up..."

Rachel decides 'gabaa' must mean a white person, but she doesn't want to interrupt Darel to ask, because she wants to know what happened to his mother.

He continues, "One night, when I was supposed to be asleep, I overheard Mum telling Dad something that had happened at school. She told him how she was trying to be friendly to the other parents when she went to Dubbo High's sport's events, assemblies and stuff, or had to drive me to a cricket or footy match at another town. She had even offered to take some other kids, if they needed a lift. Well, the mothers of the aborigines ignored her too, and one of 'em even told her to - mind her own bloody white business," when she had offered to take her son.

"You're kidding," Rachel gasps, gobsmacked. Darel shakes his head.

"I can't understand why people would be so rude to your

mother? She's such a lovely person."

"Yeah, well she gave up trying to get to know them then. Anyway, it's not like it's the first time something like that's happened to her. It's just the first time it's involved an aborigine. Some of the other white mothers that have kids at Dubbo High are the same ones from Barwon Public, so they still snob her. But, I think she got more hurt by being rejected this time because she was hoping one of the aborigine mothers might be able to tell her something about her family."

"People can be such idiots," Rachel scowls, angry at the unfair way Darel's mother had been treated.

Darel looks into her eyes, thoughtfully, before continuing. "Do you remember me telling you how Mum said she would tell me one day, what happened to her when she was little?

Rachel nods, remembering a much younger Darel, wiping tears from his eyes with the back of his hand. For some reason, she's feeling a bit nervous know.

"Well, when I overheard her telling Dad how she had been hoping to find out more about her family, it got me thinking. I had forgotten about what she had said when I was little, she'd never mentioned it since. But when that happened at Dubbo High, about her wanting to find out about her family, well, it reminded me. And then I remembered she had said something about getting lost. Then I just *had* to know - you know, what had happened when she was little? He pauses and sighs, shaking his head. "I wish I hadn't asked." He becomes silent.

Rachel reaches across and places her hand gently on top of his hand, which has been resting on the log they are sitting on. The contact breaks him from his thoughts.

"I dunno Rach. It's still hard to even think about it."

Rachel gently squeezes his hand. It must be pretty awful, what has happened to his mother. She hasn't seen him like this since that day he had last talked about it, all those years ago. If she doesn't nudge him, he might never tell her; keep it to himself. She's very curious, but should she push him to tell her something he's kept to himself all these years?

He looks so sad though, and when she'd finally told him things that made her sad, it somehow made her feel a bit better. So, surely, telling her will do the same for him. He's held onto this for over three years, for goodness sake. He's her best friend and they had grown up together. She knew more about him than anyone, probably even more than his parents, about some things.

He needs to tell her, she decides, so he can at least have someone to talk to about it.

"What happened to your Mum, Darel?"

Darel refocuses and finally blurts it out. "They took her

from her family Rach."

"What! Who took her?"

"The police, the government. White people," he spits out.

Rachel struggles to understand. "What do you mean?

"When she was just a kid, she was living with her family in the bush, somewhere in this area. The police found them and took her. She was only ten years old; well that's what they told her, anyway. She's still not sure how old she really is."

"Who told her, the police? But why did they take her?"

"No, the people from Cootamundra Home told her; the place where the police took her, where all kids like Mum were taken. They took her from her family because she was half white."

Now he's started, he's spilling it out, without pausing. "Mum said that in those days there was a law that said the people from the government could take kids like her, the ones that had one white parent. They said it was to help her to mix in with white society; give her a better chance in life. They took her to this place called Cootamundra Home, run by the mission there; religious people. She lived there, went to school there and they trained her for work. She never saw anyone from her family again, and on top of it all, she wasn't allowed to mention her family or speak any Wiradjuri words after that. She was punished if she did." He takes a big breath and expels it. "Anyway, that's how come she ended up at Jannali. A few years after she was allowed to leave the Home, she came here as a house-keeper and ended up marrying Dad."

He looks at Rachel, at her wide eyes and open mouth. He knows she is shocked by what he has just told her and he can understand why she is speechless. "Yeah, that's sort of how I reacted too when Mum told me." He sighs resignedly.

"But Darel. That…that, well, that's just — so *wrong*," she finally manages to say.

"Yeah, I know," he says disdainfully.

"I'm so sorry Darel," she says softly, a moment later, as a tear runs unchecked down her cheek.

They both continue to sit side-by-side, with their hands interlocked, staring into the river in silence, drawing comfort from each other.

CHAPTER 9

Rachel could think of little else, after her conversation with Darel about his mother. His words resounded in her mind for the remainder of that day and late into the night.

Subdued and deep in thought, she only vaguely heard her mother and father talking at the table as they ate the lamb chops, mashed potatoes, carrots and peas, and if anyone had asked her what she had eaten, she would have found it difficult to remember.

That she hadn't conversed with them, hadn't been all that unusual; her mother usually did most of the talking anyway. If she had been asked a question that night, she probably wouldn't have heard it. She found the background chatter annoying. All she wanted to do was get the evening meal and washing up over and done with, so she could retreat to her room to be alone to contemplate things in peace.

Coming to terms with what had happened to Mrs Rutherford wasn't going to be all that easy, she realises, although at least some things now made sense. Like the way Mrs Rutherford had told Darel she needed to tell him about the Wiradjuri ways, so they wouldn't get – lost. After losing everything she had always known, she could see why it was important to Mrs Rutherford to keep her memories of her family's way of life from being forgotten. And, she also now understands why she had had to keep them a secret; even the *threat* of punishment would have been enough to ensure that.

In a small way, Rachel can relate to Mrs Rutherford words about being - lost. She remembers feeling that way when she first started at Trinity. Everything had been so new and strange, and she had felt confused and powerless. But, even so, what she had felt could be nothing compared to Mrs Rutherford's experience; the way she had been taken away, not knowing where she was going, being treated the way she had at that Home, and never knowing if she would see her family again.

She tries to imagine losing her own family and being punished if she spoke her own language, or talked about the things she had learned as a child. It would be like saying; everything you know is wrong, you have to learn it all over again. Rachel likens that to brainwashing and finds it so difficult to comprehend that she actually knows someone that went through it. How could a person ever be the same again after an experience like that?

It seems amazing to her, that Mrs Rutherford is so down-to-earth and kind. She visualises Mrs Rutherford's face lighting up with a wide grin whenever she turned up at the homestead; even when it had been unplanned, such as the times she and Darel had been caught in stormy weather while playing on the Jannali side of the dividing fence. And countless times, Mrs Rutherford called her mother on the telephone to tell her where Rachel was. "We don't want your mother to worry," she would say.

There were times too, when her mother had called Mrs Rutherford to see if she were at the Jannali homestead. If she weren't, Mrs Rutherford would go searching for them, knowing she would be with Darel. She never seemed to have trouble finding them if she wanted to. But, when she found them, she would never be annoyed for having had to go searching for them in the first place, like she knows her mother would have been.

Mrs Rutherford was such an interesting person too, and her home was fascinating. Many of the rooms were filled with old furniture that reminded her of photos she had seen at the Dubbo museum. But there were also things she had never seen anywhere else, such as paintings and craft items in rich vibrant colours and unusual patterns.

Nearly every time she stepped into the house there'd be a new item. She knew they had to do with the Wiradjuri culture, so she had been careful not to say anything about them. She had been a little worried she might slip up if she said anything and somehow let on that she knew things that only Darel was supposed to know. She hadn't wanted to get Darel into trouble.

One day she came across a new painting on the wall; a beautiful rainbow which seemed to explode in the centre with birds flying from it in all directions. She had decided it was her favourite of them all, and she really wanted to tell Mrs Rutherford how much she liked it. She had just about decided that surely it wouldn't matter if she just said that, when she felt a movement at her side.

While she had been engrossed with wide-eyed delight at the myriad of colours leaping from the canvas, Mrs Rutherford had sidled up to her. When Rachel had looked up at her, Mrs Rutherford had given her a sideways hug and smiled down gently at her. Rachel had known then that she hadn't needed to tell her. They had then both stood there together in silence looking at the painting, until Darel had called her to go back outside.

When she told Darel how much she liked the new painting, he told her it had to do with a dreaming story, about how the birds got their colours from the first rainbow arch that appeared in the sky. He had then told her the story.

'*At first the arch was only fairly small, but as it began to suck in more and more red, blue, green, yellow and purple colours from all around, it started to grow and pulsate.*

Eventually, it grew so big, it exploded. The rainbow then became a million pieces that floated in the air as they slowly drifted toward the ground. And as the million colourful pieces fell towards the ground, the pieces then changed into all the birds we know today.

Some of the birds, like the crow, didn't like the feeling of falling, and they screamed out in horror, making the sound: Aaahhh, Aaahhh.

Other birds, like the kookaburra, thought it was the funniest feeling they had ever had and started to laugh, making the sound: Haahaaa, Haahaaa.

And still other birds thought it was the most wonderful feeling of all, so they spread their wings wide, opened their throats, and started to sing the most beautiful songs you could ever hear.

And that's how the birds got their colours and their voices — because of that rainbow, way back in the Dreamtime.'

That was the last dreaming story she had written in her diary. She thinks it would be so very sad if all those beautiful dreaming stories and words were lost forever. She's so glad that Mrs Rutherford has taught Darel about her mother's ways, and that she's written the stories in her diary; not just for her own remembrance, but for Mrs Rutherford and Darel's sake too.

She wonders if there were other aborigines trying to keep their ways from ever being forgotten. There must be others who felt as strongly about it as Mrs Rutherford. Then she remembers Darel's account of the aborigine boy at school who had told him to mind his own business.

Now it made sense why he had said that. Someone in his family had probably been through something similar to Mrs Rutherford. But she wonders if all aborigines had needed to keep their heritage a secret.

If it hadn't been for Darel's mother, she wouldn't know anything about aborigines, she muses. In fact, she'd had barely any contact with them other than for Mrs Rutherford; and then she was only *half* aborigine, and didn't look anything like any others she had seen, anyway.

There hadn't been any aborigines at Barwon Public School, and she had only vaguely noticed the darker-skinned people in Dubbo. She had once started a conversation with an aborigine girl though, while she had been shopping with her mother at the Dubbo supermarket. When her mother had noticed, she had literally pulled her away from the girl. When Rachel had asked her mother why she hadn't been allowed talk to her, she had just said. "Rachel, they're aborigines." When Rachel had then looked at her confused, she had added, "We don't associate with them." She had known better than to continue the discussion when her mother made statements like that.

That memory brings another to mind, about Mrs Rutherford. At school functions at Barwon Primary she had often stood quietly alone, watching things from afar, while many of the mothers had stood around talking together.

Rachel had thought it was because Mrs Rutherford must have been shy. It had never occurred to her that people would ignore her purely because she had darker coloured skin. Darel had put it down to the other mothers being snobs, even though his family were one of the more affluent families in the district.

How could she have been so blind; about so many things?

Her mother had never seemed to like Darel. Rachel had always thought it was because he was a boy, and her mother had wanted her to spend more time with girls, even though that was a silly reason not to like someone.

But, even though she now spent most of her time with girls at Trinity, she still didn't like her being with Darel. She seemed to only just manage to *tolerate* them spending time together during the school holidays.

When she had been younger her mother had never encouraged Darel to come over to the house; that's one reason why they had started to meet at the river, or went over to Darel's house.

If she had even mentioned how she had talked to Mrs Rutherford while playing with Darel on the Jannali property, her mother had looked annoyed and straight-away changed the subject.

One day, the butterfly doll Mrs Rutherford had made for

her went missing from the chair in her room. She had often taken her to bed with her so the doll was always within easy reach. She had searched everywhere, finally finding her at the back of her bedroom cupboard. When Rachel had asked her mother why she had put the doll in the cupboard, her mother had said that it was a bit of an eyesore and the beautiful porcelain doll she and her father had given her on the same birthday was far prettier to look at.

Rachel had thought she must have hurt her mother's feelings, so she then placed her butterfly doll next to her porcelain doll, side-by-side on her bookshelf. She could at least still *see* her butterfly doll there, and hoped her mother would be pleased. They were both beautiful in their own way. Couldn't her mother see that?

She realises now, if she hadn't found out about Mrs Rutherford and pieced together her memories, she could possibly have remained blind to the fact that discrimination existed in her own back yard.

Her History classes at Trinity, and even many fiction books had made her painfully aware of how people had been capable of immense cruelty; the American Indians, Negro slaves and even what Hitler had done to the Jews, came to mind. But, she had also become aware that her own country hadn't been entirely without it's cruelties to humankind either.

Australian history was focussed on the British side of things; the discovery and claim of new land needed for the establishment of a new settlement, because of the overpopulation of the goals back in England. There were detailed accounts of the progress of Australia, from the time of possession, right up until modern times.

The aborigines had been mentioned, but only in respect of having been a hindrance; primitive people, who had thwarted the new settlers in their attempts to establish civilisation in an uncivilised land. That they had resisted the attempts of the new arrivals to take their land, resulting in their deaths, had seemed inevitable to Rachel, in the overall picture of the history of the world. That was what had happened throughout history, after discovery - conquest.

The persecution of the aborigines was history, though, or so she had thought. It had happened nearly two hundred years ago; even more than a hundred a fifty years *before* the Second World War, and the atrocities that also occurred in more modern times to people in countries overseas. All that had happened a very long time before she had even been born. She had rationalised that all people must have been uncivilised back then. She couldn't ever imagine anything like that ever happening these days.

But something dreadful had happened to Darel's mother; to someone she knew; someone who was still alive. How could the Australian government have done such a thing in these modern times? And although she couldn't repeat anything she knew about Darel's mother, surely there was some way of finding out more about the aborigines.

She had already scoured the library shelves at Trinity for any information about the aborigines, without success. Even the Dubbo library had nothing other than what she had learned from her history books at Trinity. Her History teacher, Mr Weber, hadn't been helpful at all. When she had asked him about the culture of the Australian aborigines, he had just looked at her blankly, before advising her to focus on what she needed to know. How did *he* know what she *needed* to know, anyway?

It would be pointless asking her mother, now she's come to the conclusion that she'd be biased about the subject, although she still can't understand – why!

Her father, on the other hand, got on well with all the Rutherfords. Her father, yes, he would be the one to ask. He's told her things about the aborigines before. But she would need to be careful not to divulge anything about what Darel has told her. And she would need to talk to him alone somewhere, away from the house and her mother.

***

Her opportunity came the next day, when her mother was pulling ingredients from the kitchen cupboard, in preparation of baking a cake. She knew that would keep her occupied for a while.

"I'm going for a walk to the mailbox," she says, as she walks briskly out the door. She passes through the house yard gate, and veers off to the machinery shed.

She enters the shed to see her father with his head hovering over the tractor engine.

"Hi Dad."

He glances her way. "Hello Rachel."

He returns his attention to the engine. "Whatta you up to?" he asks, concentrating.

"Oh, I was just going to check the mail."

She waits for a few seconds, but as he doesn't say anything, she decides he's probably too busy to talk. She is just about to turn and leave, when he asks, "Wanna give your old man a hand?"

She walks over closer and he points to a spanner on a table close by. She hands it to him. No point beating about the bush, she decides.

"Dad, what do you know about the aborigines?"

Her father momentarily stops what he is doing, looks at her briefly and returns to the task. "Do you mean when Australia was first settled?

"No. I mean, since you've been around."

Her father is standing up now, looking directly at Rachel.

He has a fair idea why she's asking this question, half expected it, sooner or later.

"Not a lot Rachel. Well, probably about as much as most people." He looks at her and he can see by the look on her face that he's in for a conversation. He might as well get on with it. "What is it you want to know?"

"Did you have anything to do with any aborigines when you were growing up?" She thinks that's as good a place to start as any.

"No, not really. There weren't any that I know of around the Barwon district." He pauses, stroking his chin with his fingers, thinking hard. "There was this one fella I played cricket with in town though, before I met your mother. He wasn't bad with a bat as I remember. Anyway, he was a good bloke, a good sport. He kept to himself mostly...We all knew about the ones from the Mission though."

"Where was the Mission, Dad?" Rachel asks, wondering if it's the same one Mrs Rutherford went to.

"*Is*, Rachel. It's still there. It's on the other side of Dubbo; near the speed signs, going out of town. You can't see it from the road though."

"So, aborigines still live there?"

"Yes, that's where nearly all of them from Dubbo live."

She looks a little confused, so he elaborates. "There were a lot of aborigines sent to Missions long before you or I were born. And that's where they've stayed for generations. The Missions were originally set up by the Church, a long time ago, run by the government." He pauses, noticing she looks to be more satisfied now, by that answer.

"So, they were still treated differently when you were young?"

Now he knows what she's on about, although he has a feeling she knows more than she's letting on. Don had told him when Mary first became his housekeeper all those years ago, that Mary had had a rough time before arriving at Jannali. That was all he'd said though. It seems that Rachel's found out a few things about Mary, probably through Darel.

He reckoned that no matter what, Mary deserved a fair go, just like anyone else. There were others who obviously thought differently. Even though Mary was only half aborigine, it hadn't made any difference to Betty or most people in the community. They were all stuck in the same old ways. He admits though, that until Mary had become their neighbour, he hadn't given the aborigines much thought, or even paid much attention to anything he heard about them. Out of sight, out of mind.

"Well, they've pretty much been treated differently ever since the British landed in Australia. No-one can argue about that, although there will always be different opinions on the matter. You see Rachel, you can't change the past. And sometimes *wrongs* can't be *righted*. It can take a long time for people to come to terms with it too; *if* they ever do. Most of the aborigines have accepted that because they can't do anything else. They know the government is still being run by the *invaders*, as some of then call anyone who's white. But, that doesn't mean they all give up on themselves, on who they are. There are some aborigines who will never give up tryin' to make things better for their people, even if they can't make them *right* again.

Things are changing for them, even though so far it's taken a long time. For instance, in 1967, when you were seven years old, a law was finally passed to give aborigines full constitutional rights as citizens, just like any other Australian. And then in 1972, when you were twelve, Neville Bonner became a Senator, and the first aborigine to become a Member of Federal Parliament. Those were important changes for them; to help them in their fight for equality."

He decides he's probably given her enough to think about at the moment, and he needs to get the tractor fixed. "Does that clear it up a bit for you?"

Rachel nods, still absorbing her father's words. "Yeah, I think so." She leans forward and kisses him on the cheek. "Thanks Dad," she says, and saunters off to check the mail box at the front gate, deep in thought.

CHAPTER 10

"He's 'round the back verandah Don," Betty yells as she stretches her neck in an attempt to see Don's face on the other side of the rambling white rose hedge. She had glimpsed the light blue colour of his utility through the hedge as he had driven up, so she knew she wouldn't need to go out the front to greet him.

"Ta Betty," he replies unseen, and ambles along the fence and around the corner to the back house gate.

Betty sighs deeply and a worried frown returns to her face as her thoughts once more return to Bill. The doctor said he was very lucky. There was no concussion and the x-rays didn't show anything had been broken, but there was quite a lot of ligament damage which may never fully heal, he had said. "Blasted 'widow makers'," she curses out loud. The chances of walking under a tree just as a bough broke were rare, but for many people it had also been fatal. *Thank heavens it hadn't been worse,* she consoles herself, although she's still feeling a little guilty for having had those thoughts a few months back about moving into town if he should ever pass away prematurely. She wonders if she somehow caused it with her thoughts. *Don't be ridiculous, Betty,* she scolds herself.

Her train of thought is suddenly lost as she moves her position to a different section of the hedge with her pruning shears and disturbs some grasshoppers. They make her flinch as they flick away in all directions, once more causing Betty to voice her frustration. "Rotten grasshoppers," she laments. Although harmless enough on their own, when the locust swarms came, they had the potential to strip crops overnight. The Barwon community had not been spared in the winter of 1975. Bill's winter crops had been destroyed. It was part of a farmer's lot, being at the mercy of nature. Yet, despite it all, most farmers still carried on, even when drought, flood or plague hit. It was all taken in their stride.

She thinks again on the timing of it all. She can't help but feel that although the accident had been, 'the final straw that broke the camel's back', as her mother used to say, somehow it had also been a bit like divine providence too. She didn't like it that Bill was injured of course, but she doubts he would have finally made the decision otherwise, despite the lost crops and the talks they had had since Rachel was sent away. She can't help but be a little mad at him, even though things were now largely working out to her advantage. Why hadn't he mentioned what had been on his mind earlier? He had said he had been thinking about it for years. She hadn't appreciated being left out, especially when she had suffered in silence with sorting out the problem with Rachel and Darel. It was obvious Don Rutherford had known for quite a while too, though Bill had said he hadn't mentioned it to him.

She looks along the length of the hedge, satisfied for now. She turns towards the house. Time for a cuppa, she decides, and to find out if there were any new developments. *Thank goodness Rachel's not home yet,* she thinks. *We have enough to cope with at the moment.*

***

Rachel peers around the girl in front of her to look out the window, further ahead. The sign, 'Welcome to Dubbo' should be visible any moment now. The summer holidays had finally arrived. She was returning to Binda, and Darel. She could barely contain her excitement and it was impossible to keep from smiling.

This was her fourth summer holiday since first arriving at Trinity. The bus had routinely delivered her to Dubbo for all the other end of term school breaks during the last four years, but the summer holidays had always been her favourite. She could spend most of her time outside walking in the peace of the bushland around her home, swimming in the river, and spending as much time as possible with Darel.

Many of the other girls from rural areas had accepted invitations to friend's homes for part of the holidays, while others from the bush, contemplated ways in which they could spend more time in the closest town to ease the boredom of being stuck at home with nothing to do. Rachel scoffs at that thought, *nothing to do*. There was always something to do at Binda. But, that could have a lot to do with having her best friend next door, she admits.

She spots the sign and expels a lungful of air, unaware that she had been holding her breath. Not long now and the bus will pull up at the car park behind the supermarket. Her mother will be waiting beside the station wagon to take her home. She smiles, imagining meeting up with Darel this afternoon. He always seemed to know when she was coming home, and he would be waiting for her at their favourite spot by the river.

"Don't do anything I wouldn't do Rachel," Deb whispers, as if reading her mind.

"Ha! That doesn't leave me a lot to consider," Rachel jibes, smiling broadly. Debbie smirks with a feigned look of horror.

"Have a great Christmas Deb." She stands and bends down to give her friend a quick hug after the bus stops.

"You too Rachel, see ya next year," Debbie responds as she watches Rachel walk quickly down the aisle of the bus and out the door.

Rachel momentarily feels a little sad at Deb's farewell, as she also had when Jess had left the bus earlier. She loves the friendship she has with both her girlfriends from Trinity. She doesn't want to lose, either. But distance doesn't matter though when it comes to friendship, she reminds herself, thinking of Darel.

A few minutes later Rachel turns to wave to Debbie through the window, after the bus driver closes the hatch on the side of the bus from where her luggage had been removed, steps back into the bus and starts up the engine. Debbie still has another hour's travel before she reaches her destination.

Rachel stands beside her luggage and scans the car park for her mother.

"Here I am Rachel. I'm sorry I'm late. I got held up with some things," Betty Winton says breathlessly, walking up behind her.

Rachel turns around and gives her mother a smile and a quick peck on the cheek. "That's ok Mum, I've only just arrived."

Rachel and her mother transport her belongings to the car, head to the nearest Café for a milkshake, and are on the road to Binda within minutes.

The fifty minutes of travel to Barwon drag by, as Betty probes Rachel about her most recent school term at Trinity, and anything she hasn't garnered from her weekly letters.

"Have you got your certificate yet?"

"Yes Mum. It's in with my report book."

"Good, good. I want to see it when we get home."

Rachel thinks about the document contained within her report book. The heading clearly states that which she had been working towards over the last four years: New South Wales, Department of Education, School Certificate 1975. Her school and name come next: Trinity, Church of England Girls School, Orange – Rachel Elizabeth Winton, along with her student number. Lastly, her results are listed under the headings of: subject-level and grades, with her headmistress's signature at the bottom. On the reverse side there is an explanation of the grades, although she had only glimpsed at that.

She's certain her mother and father will be pleased with her results; high grades in all the subjects that matter. English, Science, Mathematics, Geography and History were all completed at an

Advanced level, with French being the only one with an Ordinary level written beside it. At least she'd passed it. She muses over that.

She had been told it was compulsory to choose a language, and her choices had either been French or German. Why would she want to learn French or German when she lived in Australia, she had questioned at the time? It wasn't as if she had any plans of living overseas, and the only French or German people she knew were her teachers anyway.

Now, if the Wiradjuri language had been a choice, it would have been so much more applicable, and definitely far more interesting. It seemed silly to Rachel that they wanted to teach her a language from the other side of the world when there were other languages that had been spoken in her own country for centuries. But, it had become obvious her opinion on this matter had not been appreciated by her French teacher, when she was asked to explain why she had wanted to know the French word for kangaroo.

That incident had not been repeated to her parents, thankfully, although her French teacher's comment in her report that term raised a query from her mother: 'Rachel could do well if she would only focus more seriously,' it had read. She can only imagine how well it would have been received by her mother, had her teacher elaborated. She had shuddered at the thought. Besides, she hadn't wanted to rock-the-boat then, because she still intended on coming home to Binda after she finished her *time* at Trinity, as she thought of it. It *had* almost felt like a prison sentence.

She had made repeated requests to be permitted to go to Dubbo High School instead, both before and after starting at Trinity. Every time she had asked though, her mother had made her thoughts on the matter, perfectly clear.

The first year had been the hardest. She had even considered running away from Trinity. However, common sense had prevailed. She only wanted to go home. It would have been futile to arrive home, only to be taken straight back to Trinity by her mother. So, she had resigned herself to the fact that she might as well try to embrace the 'Pollyanna' mentality her mother wanted her to take on, and look forward to the holidays, which would eventually come around. The next year had been a lot better. She had made friends with Jess and Deb, and although Mandy had still seemed hell bent on making her life miserable, it hadn't seemed as bad as when she had been all alone. Things had started to pick up by the third year, when she had started the Duke of Edinburgh award. At least there had been some relief then from the suffocation of the buildings and grounds of Trinity. The expeditions she had taken for the Duke of Edinburgh award had further helped her through to the completion of the fourth year and her School Certificate.

She had worked hard at her studies, tried to get on with her teachers and fellow boarders, as best she could. In truth though, she had wanted to refuse to be compliant; to let it be known to one and all that boarding school didn't suit her. But, she had behaved as was expected of her; well…mostly, anyway. Of course, she couldn't help but voice her opinion at times, even though her mother had often said she should be more self-restrained. At least she had restrained herself more than certain other girls.

Some girls in her dormitory had quickly formed into groups during the first year, and it hadn't taken long before there were at least two groups, well known by the other students as the, 'trouble makers'. Mandy was the leader of one such group. But there was also another group of girls, who cleverly concealed their activities, even from the other students. They didn't draw attention to themselves, like Mandy's group. By the fourth year, this particular 'invisible' group had honed their observation skills decidedly well. Rachel would often listen to their whispered plans as she lay trying to sleep at night, and she found herself quite impressed by the orchestration of 'the Port enterprise', in particular. When passing by the open door of the staff common room at various times of the day, a member of this group had fallen upon the idea for the perfect, 'dare'.

Each member would be dared to sneak down the spiral staircase to the staff common room and carefully remove a portion of the red liquid from the bottle labelled, Port. It was agreed by all the girls in the group that they would each observe the staff common room at various times of the day, to gather the information they first needed. It was to their advantage that the door to the staff common room was, more often than not, left wide open during the day. It was also a bonus that the staff common room was located directly below the spiral staircase; a staircase used frequently during the day by all students.

One by one, the girls reported back to the group with all the information they needed. The bottle, clearly labelled, Port, was kept in the bottom right-hand cupboard of the oak sideboard. The key to the cupboard was kept on a nail which protruded from a spot at the rear, right side, of the sideboard. And the key to the staff room was kept on the top of the doorframe after the door was locked each night.

After each girl acquired some port, and ensured both the cupboard and door were again locked, they would all assemble at the French Doors opening on to the verandah, and distribute the alcohol equally into their plastic cups. They would then giggle with delight, although with screwed up faces of disgust, as the Port was consumed. Sometimes, they would even walk out on to the aged verandah, a designated banned area due to concerns of safety, which further highlighted the thrill of their naughtiness.

They had invited Rachel on several occasions to join their group. She had been tempted at times, but remembering her pledge to herself, declined. She had kept to her plan; did what was expected, achieved good grades and avoided drawing attention as much as possible. Surely her parents would seriously consider her request to leave Trinity now. She had accomplished all that had been expected of her over the last four years, especially in regard to obtaining good results in her School Certificate. Although she had thought about little else, other than of returning to Binda, she had stopped asking her mother if she could leave Trinity soon after she had formed her plan during Second Form. But now, she had achieved what she had set out to do. It was time.

It would be futile to ask her mother if she could complete her Higher School Certificate at Dubbo High School. She's now aware that her mother would say 'no', purely on account that she wouldn't want her going to the same school as Darel. But there was always the TAFE College at Dubbo. She had seen the big sign and buildings when they had driven past it: TAFE, Technical and Further Education. Darel had even told her that he knew someone who had left High School, worked for a year, but then decided he wanted to complete the Higher School Certificate. So, he went back to TAFE to do so, and once he finished he stayed on to learn a trade. So she could finish her Higher School Certificate and then enrol in a course to train for a job, afterwards. Or, she could just start working instead.

She would be sixteen in three months, and she had her School Certificate now, so that would help her job prospects. She might even be able to take the same bus into town that Darel took to Dubbo High, until she was old enough to get her driver's licence. If she were working she could save up to buy a car; her parents couldn't argue with that. And most importantly, the reason for it all, she would be back at Binda. Now the end of Fourth Form had finally arrived, Rachel can't wait to put it to them. How can they refuse such a well thought out plan?

The small village approaches and Rachel stares out the window, watching the familiar images as they come into view. She doesn't usually pay much attention as they travel past on the way home. Instead, she usually keeps her eyes on the road ahead in anticipation of arriving at Binda, even though concentrating on the road probably doesn't make their journey any quicker. But today, she feels nostalgic.

The primary school is the first building she looks at closely; the place where she had spent the first seven years of her schooling. It looks much the same, although she notices the trees have grown and the sign out the front has been repainted.

The town hall comes next into view on her side of the car. It brings to her mind memories of annual school concerts and fancy dress balls. Across the road from it, a man is leaving the town pub, walking casually to an old beaten up utility, a black kelpie dog sitting guard in the back.

In the middle of the village, where the road forks, she looks at the small park; the stone monument in the centre surrounded by a semi-circle of rose bushes, in need of pruning. The park still only has one set of swings she notices, although there is now a water bubbler alongside. She remembers quenching her thirst on hot summer days from the tap which is still there.

The corner shop, a family business, also catering as the post office, still exhibits the faded sign from her primary school days. Even if the sign were not there, it wouldn't make any difference. Everyone knew it was where you could find most essential items without the need to drive to Dubbo. It was where you could also buy ice creams and lollies, she remembers.

The tennis courts, with their sagging outer fence, stand behind the shop. She remembers that the shop always stayed open until the last set was played underneath the bright, night lights on the tennis courts.

They pass the wheat silos, stock yards and show ground, quicker now, as her mother pushes her foot down on the accelerator and turns off to Wilson's Lane.

Seven kilometres later, along a dirt road filled with potholes, they approach the front gate of Binda. Rachel winds down her window for a clearer view of the homestead as they approach.

The car finally comes to a stop near the front house gate and she steps out and breathes deeply. She is home again.

***

"Nooo, you can't be serious?" Rachel bellows in disbelief at what her father has just told her.

"Now Rachel, I know you don't like the idea, but the decision has been made and you will just have to accept it," her father attempts to cut off any further emotional outbursts.

"Oh Dad, I'm so sorry you're *hurt*, you know that, but can't you get someone to help until you're better? Because, I know you'll get better Dad. I just know it," Rachel pleads.

"Rachel it's not only because your father is injured," Betty intercedes. "There's a lot more to it than that..." she pauses, considering if she should elaborate, but Rachel jumps in before she can make up her mind.

"I can leave boarding school, come help Dad. I'll be sixteen soon, and...oh..." This is not going at all how she had envisaged. She panics and looks around the room frantically, searching for words.

"Rachel, you will *not* be leaving Trinity. You have two more years left yet, and then, well, we've been looking at universities..." Betty interjects.

Rachel looks defiantly at her mother. "I don't want to go to uni Mum. I don't want to leave Binda. I can't leave Da..." She stops abruptly mid-sentence, noticing the look on her mother's face and her father raising his hand to rub his temple, and she knows it's pointless. She suddenly gasps with a sob, turns and flees out the back door.

"Rachel...come back here, *now!*" her mother yells sternly after her.

"Let her go Betty," Bill says softly. "Give it a chance to sink in. It's been a big shock to her."

Betty grimaces and sits down beside Bill at the kitchen table. "Well, we had to tell her straight away, before *Darel* told her, to let her get used to the idea and make the most of what will most likely be her last summer here."

Bill reaches across and pats her hand resting on the table. "Just let her think it's all because of me. I don't want her blaming herself for not being a boy, or have to explain to her why it's best for *her* future," he adds, looking at her firmly, with raised eyebrows.

"Well, I can't see her accepting it gracefully, one way or the other. Although, if *that* boy next door wasn't in the picture, she might have," Betty adds, avoiding Bill's dig at her.

"Hmm, I dunno. Anyway, hopefully she'll have a change of heart once she has all the diversions of Dubbo, during the holidays. She just hasn't known any different. Rachel's a good girl; she'll eventually come 'round," Bill says, trying to convince them both.

***

Rachel only stopped running when she arrived at the river bend. Her head was spinning and her lungs felt like they would burst. Sobs racked her body as she picked up a handful of pebbles and hurled them angrily into the river, repeating the action until her arm ached.

"Why, oh why …?" she moans, glancing up to the tree-tops as if to find her answer there, whispering in the breeze. "Why is this happening?" she asks pitifully as she collapses onto a log and with pain etched on her face stares earnestly into the water.

"Rach, please don't cry." Darel's voice causes Rachel to turn to see him standing behind her, with sadness in his eyes.

Rachel can't help but smile softly through her tears and quickly attempts to wipe the wetness away from her cheeks with her fingertips. She pats the log, beckoning him to sit beside her.

Darel has changed in the last few months. As she watches him walk to the log and sit, she notices he has grown taller, and the muscles in his arms have developed even more since last spring. He watches her appraising him, and deliberately meets her eyes, then slowly sweeps his eyes down her body, and back up again to her face. She blushes, and turns to look intently at the water ahead while she gains her composure.

"So, you know then?" she says somberly.

"Yeah…a few weeks now."

"I just don't understand Darel. How can they leave Binda, just like that? It's our *home*."

"I know Rach, it's hard to understand," he offers gently. He looks intently at her as if he is about to say more, but changes his mind and looks away.

"What?" Rachel asks frowning.

"I don't know if you want to hear it Rach."

"Well you won't know until you tell me, will you?"

Once again, he looks at her, deliberating before continuing. "It's what Mum would say; about the land, *garray*."

Rachel nods in acknowledgement, hoping he will say something that will somehow offer some comfort, though she can't imagine anything doing that at the moment.

"Well, Mum says the land owns us, not the other way around. She still believes what she was taught as a girl; that we're meant to look after the land, not own it. So, even if you don't own it anymore Rach, you'll still always be a part of it." He pauses and looks at her intently, noticing that her demeanour hasn't altered. "But, I guess that doesn't help much at the moment."

"No, it doesn't," she says flatly. "We're still going, and I won't be able to come back." Her lips tremble.

"Yes you will." Darel says adamantly, and straightaway bites his tongue.

Rachel frowns, frustrated, growing angry. "Spit it out Darel. Why did you say that? You're confusing me."

"Oh damn, I didn't want to tell you. I knew you'd get mad."

"Darel Rutherford, if you don't tell me what you're holding back, I swear I'll...I'll...oh, I don't know what I'll do but...," she begins exasperated.

"Rach, Dad's buying Binda," he says, interrupting.

Rachel stares at Darel, unable to comprehend what he has just said. Darel looks at her with concern in his eyes.

"Rach, you know you'll always be welcome here. I will always….."

Rachel stands abruptly and looks down at Darel sitting on the log. "I don't believe this is happening," she responds quietly, in disbelief. "So, you and your father are in on it too?" She turns to walk away, but Darel is in front of her in an instance, pinning her arms firmly to her sides.

"Rach, I know you can't understand at the moment, but..." he begins.

She glares at him. "Let go of me Darel."

Darel drops his arms to his side and looks imploringly into her eyes, waiting for her to speak.

"No, I *can't* understand Darel. I *can't* understand how you could be a part of this. I thought we were best friends. I thought we would always...," her face contorts as she attempts to hold back her tears.

Darel reaches for her, and this time she relinquishes and falls unashamedly into his arms.

From the moment her parents told her the news, she has felt like the whole world is against her. She hasn't had a chance to put forward her plan to them. It had been squashed, even before they even knew about it. It was useless now. Then, while she's still trying to wrap her head around the fact that she's about to lose her home, Darel tells her *his* family are buying it. She's so angry at her parents, at Darel's parents, at everyone.

She can't seem to get a grip on her emotions, and especially now Darel is holding her in his arms. She wants to be angry with him too, but he seems to be drawing all the anger from her in his embrace.

He tilts her head backwards with the tip of his finger under her chin, looks deeply into her emerald green eyes, and his heart almost breaks. He can hardly bear to see the sadness in their depth. He bends his head, closes his eyes and places his lips upon hers, gently parting their softness, trying desperately to transfer the strength of his love into her.

"It's gunna be alright Rach," he whispers into her hair a short moment later, as he holds her firmly against him.

Rachel suddenly goes rigid, and pushes him away. Though still trembling inwardly from the sweet experience of her first kiss, she looks calmly at Darel and says, "You said that just before I first left for boarding school Darel. I believed you then, but now, I'm not so sure."

She turns and walks off defiantly, along the riverbank.

CHAPTER 11

Miss Pritchard sits behind the huge, ornate mahogany desk, and watches Rachel walk towards her. Rachel tries with every bit of willpower she has to look away, at anything, other than to meet the eagle eyes of her headmistress staring at her.

At first she succeeds, looking to her right and then to her left, with an air of nonchalance she somehow manages to pull off. If she weren't deliberately attempting to avoid those eyes, she would actually find this room quite fascinating and enjoy looking at it more closely. It looks like it had initially been decorated in the last century and remained untouched ever since.

Closed, rich red velvet drapes adorn the window to her right, giving the room a secretive atmosphere. Directly in front of the window, a plush leather three-seater settee, and a matching single chair are positioned ready for visitors. Rachel remembers sitting on that settee at her first interview just over four years ago. However, the only other thing she remembers is her headmistress's penetrating eyes making her feel uncomfortable.

A floor to ceiling mahogany bookcase completely fills the

length of the wall opposite the window, interrupted only by a closed-in white marble fireplace. A tapestry covered chair, oak side table and matching lampstand stand in front of the fireplace.

Her perusal has lasted little more than the time it has taken to walk the length of the royal blue carpet runner to reach the desk, but as she returns her gaze to Miss Pritchard, she is acutely aware that she has not been impressed.

"Rachel Winton," Miss Pritchard states as she scrutinizes Rachel over the top of her black rimmed glasses.

"Well?"

"Yes, Miss Pritchard?" Rachel answers politely.

"Rachel, it's come to my attention that your grades have dropped dramatically this term. Why is that?"

"I don't know Miss Pritchard," she replies and bites her tongue between her teeth.

Miss Pritchard frowns, looks down at the paperwork in front of her and back up to Rachel. She tries a different approach. "Rachel, for the last four years you have been a model student. You have always taken home an end-of-term report showing consistently higher than average marks for every subject, and nothing but praise from your teachers *and* myself for your very good behaviour and commitment to your studies. However, for some reason that will not be the case this term." She pauses, to see if her words have had any effect on Rachel, and as there is no noticeable change in Rachel demeanour, she continues... "Rachel, this is a very important year for you. In fact, the next two years will be. The effort you put into them will have a huge bearing on your future once you leave Trinity."

Rachel flinches, and Miss Pritchard feels she is finally getting somewhere. "What have your parents planned for you once you leave Trinity?"

Rachel looks down suddenly at her feet. Miss Pritchard has hit on a nerve and she is trying to compose herself before she answers.

Miss Pritchard purses her lips in impatience and raises her eyebrows questioningly. "Don't make me ask you again Rachel."

Rachel looks up. "My parents want me to go to Canberra, Miss Pritchard. They are considering the Australian National University."

"Ah yes, a good choice." She looks down at the paperwork in front of her again and straightens the pile before looking back sharply at Rachel. "Well, whatever the reason has been for your unusual results and behaviour this term, you will need to rectify it, immediately. You will also need to apply yourself diligently from now on to make up for your lapses this term. I hope you now realise that you cannot avoid your responsibilities if you are to make your parents proud and do well at university. Don't allow yourself to be distracted from pursuing your goals." Miss Pritchard says sternly and waits for a response.

"Yes, Miss Pritchard," Rachel responds accordingly, and with a flick of her hand Miss Pritchard indicates that the discussion has ended and Rachel turns and walks promptly from the headmistresses office.

"I said my parents *want* me to go to university. I didn't say I was *going to*," Rachel mutters under her breath as soon as she is out of earshot of the general office area next to Miss Pritchard's office.

She is meant to return to History class now, but instead, heads to her dormitory hoping no one sees her. She just can't stand the idea of explaining to Mr Weber that her lateness was because she had been summoned to the Head Mistress's office. She imagines the smug expression on his face if she had to tell him that. He had never liked her question about the aborigines and seemed to pounce on her every time she questioned anything he said after that. How could she find out what she wanted to know if she didn't ask questions?

What's the point of learning about history, anyway, if it's only one-sided? Hardly anything is written about the aborigines in Australia; about *their* history which must go back at least some time before the British arrived. So it stands to reason that there would be countless unknown cultures in the world also. What of *their* history? How can you call it World History when it doesn't include - the *whole* world? By rights, they should call it: World History – The Known Bits! She understands the aborigines didn't record things the way white people do, but she doesn't want to excuse anyone, for anything, at the moment. She's just angry, and somehow that anger is helping her to keep it together.

And then there's religion. It doesn't make sense either. Darel has taught her about the dreaming, about becoming part of the land after death, and yet the school minister preaches about going to heaven, if you don't end up in hell. She knows there are many different religions and beliefs in the world, but, if they're *all* right, who's to know what really happens once we die anyway, unless the leaders of all the religions of the world have returned from the dead to tell us. She feels like they're all trying to brainwash her. Why can't they just let her work it out for herself? She has after all, already worked out on her own, that there is a difference between religion and spirituality; one is taught - religiously, the other experienced - freely. So far, experience has been the best teacher. She smirks at the irony of that.

To top it off, her mother has written to inform her that she can no longer return to Binda now because the sale of the property has been finalised. She told her that she had already packed up all her belongings and from the next term break she would be coming to their new home in Dubbo. She described their new home in detail and all the things she can do now she'll be living there. She then mentioned that they had bought a business in town too. Well, that letter had been ripped to shreds straight after reading it.

Two more years at Trinity are going to seem even longer than the last four. Yet now, she's not looking forward to what's expected of her after that either. If her mother has her way she'll be sent away to university, even further away from Binda and Darel; to learn more about things that seem so irrelevant to her.

Everything is so messed up. She thought she only had to get through Trinity and then everything would get better again. That if she did her best and made her parents proud, they would be more willing to listen to her, care how she felt. Wasn't good behaviour supposed to be rewarded?

She understands that her parents sold Binda because her father couldn't work the land anymore. She feels sorry for her father. If only she had been a boy. At sixteen, she would be like Darel, helping her father. Darel hadn't had a chance to tell her that he finished up at Dubbo High after he completed his School Certificate. She had left him at the river that day after he had kissed her, and avoided him for the remainder of the holidays. She had been walking to the bathroom one night afterwards and overheard her father telling her mother how he had finished up at school so he could help his father full-time now they had Binda to work as well. She had felt like someone had kicked her in the stomach. Although she never imagined she wouldn't see him again after that day, she had felt unable to trust anyone at that time. She even found it difficult to trust her own emotions.

No-one seems to care what she thinks or feels anyway. Even Darel had a 'she'll be right' attitude the last time she saw him. Those last words he spoke to her: 'It's gunna be alright', echo in her mind, taunting her. It was easier for him. He didn't have to leave Jannali. She feels like it must be a bad dream, a nightmare. If only someone would wake her up.

Binda is no longer her home and even though she still can't stop thinking of Darel, she's so confused about him now. She wants desperately to be angry with him, but her resolve repeatedly lets her down, especially at night when she's remembering... Her heart says one thing, her mind another. Well, she knows how well following her heart had worked, where it had got her. Yet, no matter what, she now knows she is powerless about changing any of it, so what's the point in trying? But, wasn't it that very same attitude which had come to Miss Pritchard's notice? Maybe the answer is staring her in the face. She couldn't change the fact that her home was now lost to her, and most likely Darel, but perhaps she had already found a way to get out of going to university.

CHAPTER 12

Rachel studies herself in the full-length mirror on the wall outside her dormitory, paying close attention to the bodice of her new long, emerald green, dress. She smiles, wondering if anyone will notice. She's sure Jess will.

As if appearing in answer to her name being spoken out loud, Jess abruptly pokes her head around the corner and Rachel jumps, laughing.

"Stop gawking at yourself Rachel. You look good."

"Thanks, but take a better look. Some girlfriend you are," she baits, disappointed.

"What? I told you earlier how envious I am of that dress. It's gorgeous. And I love the way it matches your eyes."

"No, that's not it...look clos-er," Rachel grins as she places her hands on the silky green material beneath her firm young breasts, and lifts them up for perusal."

"Rach-el," Jess squeals. "What's the go with that? Oh, you haven't...?"

With raised eyebrows and a smirk, Rachel nods.

"Oh, I must admit, you do now look so so-phis-ti-cated," Jess teases, slipping her arm through Rachel's as they saunter down the stairs.

"How many tissues did you use?" she whispers, giggling, as they navigate the winding staircase to the front foyer where Miss Bart will inspect them from top to toe, before permitting them out the front door and onto the bus.

"Ssshh," Rachel warns; their conversation quickly stalled as they reach the bottom of the steps and Miss Bart enters the foyer.

"Attention girls," Miss Bart bellows. "Line up and walk decorously past me to the bus please."

As the room full of girls step individually through the front doorway, Miss Bart examines them from head to toe, checking dress lengths, footwear, and for signs of any excessive make-up. After the last dance, no-one wants to be held responsible for keeping the bus waiting, to be the one ordered to race upstairs to scrub off bright coloured lipstick or change stiletto heels for something more practical.

Mandy had found out the hard way, at the last dance, that the other girls didn't appreciate her over-the-top applications when it delayed their much-anticipated night out. She had received steely stares from many of the girls as she took a seat on the bus, once Miss Bart finally granted her access.

Every school term, the girls of Trinity attend a 'dance' with one of the other private all-boy boarding schools in

Orange. That is, as long as they have no demerits points against their name at the time, and are suitably attired. Rachel thinks it's nothing short of a miracle she hasn't been denied going to this dance because of her apparent misbehaviour this term. The tissues obviously didn't work either. *I guess stuffing your bra with tissues isn't considered unladylike*, Rachel concludes. *I should have come up with something better.*

It was the last social event for the term and the first senior dance for Rachel's class. It was normally a very exciting event for the girls in Fifth Form, but Rachel had wanted to get out of going, and she thought the tissue idea might work. Miss Bart hadn't even looked at her properly. Lately she had started to feel like she was becoming invisible at Trinity too.

It's not that she wants to encourage any boys with her tissued packed bra. She had always discouraged them as much as possible in the past. Even from the time of her very first dance when she was a junior, she had remained as much as possible in the background. It had become easier once Jess and Deb came along. The girls would dance together if they weren't asked by a boy, so she had still been able to enjoy herself, while remaining unavailable. It was relatively easy to pretend to be tongue-tied if a boy approached, and that was how she managed to shift the focus from herself to her girlfriends. She was more than happy to step back and let her girlfriends test their social skills with the boys.

As same-sex schools, contact between the girls and boys was generally restricted to junior and senior social dances, joint ballroom dance classes, sporting events and concerts held at the town's Civic Centre. Saturday and Sunday afternoon visits, exchanging of letters via posted mail and visits to one another's homes during school breaks, followed the more serious romances that developed. Some liaisons formed during the last years of senior school ended up becoming long term relationships years later; sometimes even marriage.

The senior girls at Trinity enjoy the dances much more when they are held at one of the boy's schools. The girls have discovered that the wily Miss Bart is often not as observant at the boy's school as she is in her own familiar school surroundings.

The bus makes its way to its destination, illuminated by the streetlights in the night. Some of the occupants are wistfully lost in their own thoughts, silently wishing for cupids arrow to find its way to them tonight. Other girls, already 'taken', however, are smiling in anticipation of being held close during the dances, and perhaps receiving a stolen kiss afterwards.

"You don't need those, you know", Jess whispers sideways, pointing to Rachel's chest. "And why would you want Martin drooling over you even more, when you ignore him all the time, anyway?"

"Hmm, I dunno. Maybe I'm a bad person."

Jess frowns and then admonishes her. "Oh Rachel, haven't you had enough of being a fake yet? You don't fool me. Besides, if you don't stop thinking about Darel, you'll probably really need those tissues to get noticed when you're older," she braves.

Rachel opens her mouth to argue with Jess's words but closes it with a scowl. She knows her best friend means well, despite being annoyed by her words. However, she also knows she's right in at least one respect. She'll never be able to get Darel out of her mind, no-matter how hard she tries. He would always be an important link to her past, an integral part of her childhood happiness at Binda. He had been her best friend and confidante growing up in a small community, living in semi-isolation. And, even if any of those were valid enough reasons to keep him in her memory, he had also been the first boy she had ever kissed.

She shouldn't have pushed him away that day, and stormed off. The kiss had felt so natural to her, like it was something she had been expecting all along, without even knowing it. She will never forgive herself for deliberately avoiding him.

Once she had found out that he had started working with

his father full-time, she had chosen to visit their favourite place by the river during the day, instead of during the evenings, when he would have had the opportunity to meet her there.

She had been so confused about so many things. Had he only kissed her because he had felt sorry for her? Had it been his way of saying, goodbye? The hurt about losing her home had been too bitter to chance that also being the case with Darel. She wanted to savour that kiss, again and again and believe it had been genuine. Staying away from him had seemed like the only way to ensure it in her mind.

She hadn't been able to help herself though on her last evening at Binda before going back to Trinity. She had walked down to the river, hoping to see him. She had wanted the chance to find out for certain, while her heart wasn't feeling as vulnerable as it had before. But, Darel hadn't turned up. Was it because she had stayed away repeatedly the entire summer, or had he decided to deliberately stay away also?

The last four years had been tough for Rachel, but she knows they would have been a great deal tougher, if it hadn't been for Binda and Darel, and also, Jess. Jess is the best of friends. What if Jess is right? As much as she finds it almost unbearable to think of, what if Darel really doesn't care for her anymore, and she winds up pining for him her whole life?

She's not even sure if she'll ever see him again now anyway.

Rachel sneaks a look at Jess sitting solemnly beside her, reaches down into the cups of her bra and pulls the tissues out.

"You're right," she says, shoving the tissues between the seat and the window. "I don't need these, and I need to start looking elsewhere," she adds, nearly choking on her words.

As soon as they enter the dance venue, Rachel notices the couples pairing up and nearly jumps when a voice whispers tentatively beside her.

"Hi Rachel." Martin stands beside her, blushing.

Rachel glances at Jess gazing nonchalantly around the room, with a smirk on her face.

"Hi," she replies, smiling, while skilfully throwing her leg behind her as she turns to face him directly, and deliberately kicks Jess.

"Ouch," Jess grimaces, but discretely ambles away when she spots Deb's boyfriend walking towards her with a questioning look.

After hearing that his girlfriend is in sick-bay with a bad cold, his face drops, but Jess soon has him smiling again, and they walk off together towards a group of boys.

The music starts, and the school hall is suddenly filled with the rustling of feet everywhere in last minute dashes to procure a partner.

Rachel looks over to see Jess laughing gaily with a boy she has never seen before. The girls and boys, who have partnered up to dance, move into the centre of the room. 'Daddy Who', booms from the speakers positioned either side of the stage.

Martin looks directly into Rachel's eyes and starts to sway back and forth in time to the music. Rachel follows suit and soon they're dancing joyfully to Skyhooks reminding them that they're 'Living In The Seventies', followed by 'Band On The Run'.

Rachel is enjoying herself. Martin's not a bad dancer, she decides. He really is kind of cute too, with his wavy, sandy coloured hair. It reminds her of the salt and pepper coloured sand banks along the river at Binda.

Much later, as the music slows, drawing to the end of the night, Martin takes the opportunity he's been waiting for. For many months now, he's jumped at every chance to talk to Rachel, and dreamed every night of holding her in his arms. Rachel has always been nice to him, but he's often felt when he's talking to her that she's lost in thought, aloof, and far away. She's not like any other girl he knows. She enchants him with her golden hair, emerald green eyes and wistful, dreamy expression. Tonight however, he's noticed a change in her. She seems to have lifted that invisible veil she's always hidden behind. He feels encouraged by her small smiles and gentle touches, as she walks with him to the refreshment table. Right now, he would do anything to be able to hold her.

Elton John, serenades, 'Don't Go Breaking My Heart', and he bravely opens his arms, in invitation. Rachel pauses ever so slightly before moving into his embrace. His heart pumps wildly as he holds her close and they sway as one to the beat. When 'Bridge Over Troubles Waters', becomes the last dance for the night, she looks up searchingly into his melting, smoky brown eyes as he eagerly lowers his lips to hers.

***

Rachel draws back from Martin's kiss and smiles gently.

"Do you remember the first time you kissed me?" she asks.

Martin grins. "How could I ever forget it? Of course, it had nothing to do with No-Heart Bart tapping me on the shoulder at the same time." He chuckles.

"I kind of feel a bit sorry for her though you know." Rachel bites her bottom lip.

"What! I thought she gave you hell, for years."

"Yes, but I gave her a hard time back, when I was older," she admits openly.

Martin raises his right eyebrow with a stern expression.

Rachel laughs and slaps him playfully. "Stop teasing."

"Ok, fess up. What did you do to your old House Matron that was so bad?"

"Well...," she begins grinning, and contorts her mouth. "She had a hearing aid, and sometimes I started answering her questions without speaking. Only move my mouth silently in reply. She would get so confused and try desperately to discretely turn her aid up. Then, once I knew she had it up really loud, I'd answer her again. It must have hurt her ears."

Martin laughs loudly. "And you always looked so meek and vulnerable. I had no idea you were capable of such naughtiness," he scolds.

Rachel sighs. "Yes, that place sure changed me."

Martin senses troubled ground and quickly changes the subject, while stroking her back.

"Do you know, after that first kiss, I couldn't concentrate for weeks? I even walked into the wrong dorm that night afterwards; I was in such a trance. You made my dream come true." He looks at her with adoration.

She gently caresses his cheek with her fingertips. "It was a night I'll never forget either Martin," she says softly, hating herself. She carefully pulls away from his embrace, looks at her watch and exclaims, "I have work soon. Remember, *some* people actually *work*," she teases.

"Such the comedian today, aren't we," he jokes, grabbing

her by the arm, pulling her close against his chest.

"I'll be late if you keep this up," she says, pretending to be mad.

"Ok, ok, I concede, but only because you look so beautiful. I'll go bug Johno. I'll see you later. Six thirty?"

Rachel smiles at him as he saunters back to his dark green Fiat, whistling, and drives off. She settles herself back onto the grass overlooking the pond at the park, where they've just shared a picnic lunch. She still has a few minutes before she's due at the store.

She thinks back to her first kiss with Martin. Yes, although over two years ago now, she would certainly never forget it. She would never forget it, because even though she had tried so hard not to, she'd been thinking of Darel, and wishing it were him.

CHAPTER 13

"Hi Dad," Rachel says as she walks into the office and sits down quickly at the desk.

"Oh Good, I'm off home for lunch, now you're here. Kevin's out the back, but Matt's on a delivery. Roger Tarrant will be coming in some time this 'arvo to pick up some seed. The order's there," he points to the tray in front of her.

Rachel sighs. "Yes Dad, I'll manage. Off you go," she says, smiling.

Bill grins. "Yes, I know you will. He gives her a pat on the shoulder. "I'm glad you're here Rachel," he says as he walks out the door, but pokes his head back in abruptly. "Have the new brochures arrived yet?" Rachel nods. "Good. Make sure you give one to Rodg when he comes."

"Yes Dad, now go have some lunch." His head disappears and she is finally alone.

Yes, Rachel thinks, *I'm glad I'm here too*. She was enjoying working alongside her father, even if it was in a store instead of at Binda.

The previous owner of 'Wallis & Co', Bob Wallis, had taught her father the ropes when he first took the farm produce store over from him just over two years ago. Bob had stayed on as co-manager for the first six months. It had been a good arrangement for her father. Having been a farmer all his life, managing a store was a huge change, but he had seemed to take to it like a duck to water. It was an added bonus when the two other employees, Kevin Cross and Matt Pilon stayed on with the change of ownership.

Kevin had been with the business since the original owner, Harold Wallis, Bob Wallis's father, had been in charge. "I was only a young'un when I came to work for Old Man Wallis," he'd told Rachel. Bob had employed Matt soon after he had taken over the ropes, because they had needed another set of hands when Old Man Wallis retired.

It was still a reasonably small business, although over the years it had earned a good reputation and regular business with several of the local farmers, particularly around the Barwon area where Harold Wallis had originally farmed the land before moving to Dubbo. Kevin and Matt kept things rolling as they always had in the store front and docks.

Rachel was only working part-time at Wallis & Co, while she completed her secretarial studies at Dubbo TAFE. She liked it; being close to her father and in contact with farmers. Just like her father does, she realises.

It was obvious he enjoyed managing the store, having a chat with the farmers who came in for supplies, many of whom he knew from Barwon. As the doctor had said, his back had never fully healed, and he sometimes needed to go home for a rest. He didn't let it get him down though and as soon as he could, he'd be back at the store, smiling and joking as if he didn't have a care in the world. But, there was always someone from the Winton family at the store. If her father needed to go home, her mother would still be there working the morning shift, until Rachel arrived after classes at TAFE to work the afternoon shift.

Just like her father had learned the ropes from Mr Wallis, her mother had taken over the administrative tasks from Mrs Wallis, but after only a few weeks of training. Her mother was a fast learner. Rachel imagines she should be, having been a teacher.

By the time Rachel had completed her Higher School Certificate, the business was running as smooth as a well-oiled machine. Yes, going to TAFE and working at Wallis & Co was helping her to manage the empty feeling she still felt within her heart. And although she's not sure if she'll ever be able to forgive her mother for depriving her of all those years she could have had at Binda and with Darel, by being sent to Trinity, she is grateful that at least she hadn't insisted she go to university in Canberra. Well, in reality, she had coerced her mother to allow her to stay. She doubts she will ever be forgiven for that, but she really doesn't care.

At the end of the first term of her final two years at Trinity, she brought to her new home at Dubbo, the worst report card she had ever received. Her mother was horrified, not only by her marks, but by the comments from her teachers and the headmistress about her conduct. However, after the initial shock had worn off, instead of making a big deal about it as Rachel had expected, she sobered and instead, had shown quite a reserved concern. Rachel had begun to worry that her efforts to make a point had been to no avail; that was, until the anticipated conversation with her mother, eventually came.

"Rachel, I understand it's been a big change for you, moving to Dubbo, but you really must try to concentrate on your studies, especially now that you're getting so close to your Higher School Certificate."

"Is it really that important Mum?" she asks decisively.

"Yes Rachel, of *course* it is. You need to achieve good grades to get into university."

"But I don't want to go to uni Mum," she responds firmly, yet again.

Betty sighs. "Don't you want to end up with a good job Rachel, a career, before you marry and have children?"

"Mum, what's the point of having a career if I'm only going to get married and have children anyway, one day. I can get a job without going to uni. There are lots of other options. I could go to TAFE and learn secretarial studies or even help Dad out at the store; take over from you?"

Betty grimaces. "Well…it's not what I had in mind for you Rachel. I didn't send you to Trinity so you could wind up working in a store."

"So, it's good enough for you and Dad, but not me?" Rachel braves. "If I had been a boy Mum, we'd probably still be at Binda, and I'd be keeping the farm going for Dad. Maybe I could take over from Dad in the store one day instead, seeing I couldn't do that at Binda."

"Rachel, you do like to push me to my limits, don't you?" Betty says exasperatedly, biting her tongue to avoid exposing the additional reasons why they had sold Binda. In a way, she feels Rachel has her backed into a corner, but there could be some merit in her suggestion. "Well, your father and I will need to discuss it. *But*, in the meantime, we know you are more than capable of improving your marks, *and* your behaviour. Goodness Rachel, this is not – *you*," she frowns as she waves the report book in her hand. She then looks at Rachel intently, thinking quietly. "I guess there could be other options to going to university, although I can't understand why you don't want the opportunity it will offer you." she adds quietly, and pauses, her mind obviously whirling. "Well, as I said, your father and I will talk about it, but I'm sure he will agree with me that we'll need to see you making more of an effort, in either respect."

It had worked! Rachel had again, applied herself diligently to her studies, and improved her behaviour at Trinity. Her parents had been duly proud when she had received her Higher School Certificate with flying colours, at the end of Sixth Form.

She had even achieved the Gold Award in the Duke of Edinburgh scheme for completing a four-day and three-night expedition, along with the on-going, physical recreation, skill and service, time requirements. However, unlike the two previous awards, the Gold Award had also included voluntary work of five-days and four-nights, staying in an unfamiliar environment.

Jess had pleaded with Rachel to join her to complete this activity at the Prince Alfred Hospital, in Sydney. Rachel couldn't for the life of her understand where Jess had developed this sudden yearning to work as a nurse, not ever having mentioned it to her before. However, it soon became apparent once they were settled into the nurse's quarters that Jess's desire for the caring profession had largely stemmed from somehow knowing they would be able to sneak out at night to experience the night life of Sydney. It had been quite an eye-opener for two seventeen-year-old girls from the country, though Rachel had been relieved when they had left the city far behind them.

Her mother had reminded her that she was quite capable of doing well at university, after her achievements at Trinity. She had even hinted that it wasn't too late to change her mind. Thankfully, this time, her father had come to her rescue. "Rachel is joining us at Wallis & Co, and that's all there is to it Betty," he had said.

Rachel finishes printing off the monthly invoices just as she hears a vehicle pulling up at the main door, shed entrance. That must be Roger she thinks. She quickly stands, walks over and opens the door to the cupboard where she put the new brochures when they arrived yesterday. Hidden behind the cupboard door, she hears the office door open. "Be right there Mr Tarrant," she says, pulling out a brochure from the box and closing the door.

She turns, looks to the doorway, straight into Darel's eyes. "Hello Rach."

Time stands still and she realizes she is staring. "Hi Darel," she finally responds.

"So, you really *are* working here with your Dad?"

"Yeah. It's funny how things work out sometimes, isn't it?" Her heart is thumping, and his blue eyes feel like they're piercing her soul.

Silence, and then they both turn as they hear another vehicle arrive. Darel turns to see Roger Tarrant walking up behind him. Rachel finally reclaims her senses. "Oh, hello Mr

Tarrant, I'll be right with you," she says, looking past Darel. Returning her gaze to Darel, she asks softly, "Is there something I can help you with Darel?"

"Yes Rach. Always!" He pauses. "But it can wait for a bit longer. I'll call back another time." He grins, turns and nods to Roger Tarrant. Rachel watches, stunned, as he walks to his beige coloured HT Belmont utility she can see through the open door at the back of the shed, and drives away.

Rattled by Darel's surprise visit, she somehow manages to assist Roger Tarrant, although she forgets to give him the brochure.

***

Martin reaches across the table and takes her hand. She looks up and forces a smile.

"Are you ok?" he asks, looking concerned.

"Yes, I'm fine," she says, trying to remain smiling. "I guess I'm just a little tired."

"We can go if you like."

Rachel nods, "If you don't mind. I think I'd like an early night."

Martin drops her off at home arranging to see her the next day. She shouldn't have spoiled their dinner by feigning tiredness, but she doesn't feel that bad because she knows he'll be off to find Johno at the pub. They'll play pool and drink until the pub closes, and stager back to Johno's flat, where they'll pass out until tomorrow's morning sun glares at them through the blinds.

Martin was by nature quite a reserved person, a perfect gentleman. Rachel finds it strangely liberating at times to see or imagine him 'letting his hair down' from time to time, with his friend who he went to boarding school with. He's a uni student now, so in a way it's kind of expected anyway by the stories he tells her. Thinking of boarding school friends reminds her of Jess. She decides to get in touch and invite her for a visit, now she's settled into TAFE and working at the store.

She walks to the corner of the verandah, and sits on the swinging chair hanging from the roof. It's such a beautiful night. She looks up to the sky. It's a full moon. She imagines watching it from the verandah of Binda, and imagines Darel looking up at it as well. He once told her that the name of his home, 'Jannali', means 'place of the moon', so looking at the moon had always been a nightly ritual for him. She had then asked him if he knew what 'Binda' meant, and he had promptly replied, 'deep water'. He said he had overheard his mother and father talking about it on the back verandah one night. "Mum said there's been a lot of tears cried at the river, and that's why it's so deep."

Yes, Darel had caused her to come home early tonight. She just couldn't stop thinking about his visit at the store today. It had been two and a half years since she had last seen him. He would be eighteen now, just like her, although he could easily pass for twenty, she thinks. He had only stood in front of her for a few moments, but the image of him with his broad strong shoulders and sun bronzed good looks had remained in her mind, immovable, all afternoon and night.

The front door opens and her father joins her on the verandah. "You're home early, everything alright?"

"Yes Dad. I just wanted an early night." She feels guilty.

"Nothin' wrong with that; your mother was wondering," he says glancing behind him to make sure he was alone. "Sent me out to investigate, but don't tell her I told you," he whispers with a grin.

She smiles knowingly, and relaxes. "Darel came into the store today Dad. It's the first time I've seen him since I was last at Binda."

"Is it? Well, he's been in a lot since you started working with me these last six months. I would've thought you'd have seen him by now."

"Hmmm, I guess he's called in when I've been at TAFE, when Mum's been there...Did *you* tell him I was working there now?"

"Not Darel, 'though I do remember telling Don. He often asks after you. He would've told him I reckon," Bill looks at her thoughtfully. "Well, I've been out here long enough to be able to tell your mother that you and Martin didn't have a blue. You didn't, right?"

She rolls her eyes at him. "No Dad. You can tell Mum everything's ok." It's times like this she wishes she had her own flat, but then she thinks of Martin, and reconsiders. It's probably a good thing she can't afford it just yet.

"Ok, then." He pats her shoulder affectionately and goes back inside, leaving her with a troubled mind.

Her mother wanted to know absolutely everything concerning Martin. It had almost seemed like it had become her new mission in life. That was, when she wasn't talking about her involvement in various community organisations in Dubbo, or her new friends. Yes, her mother had settled in well at Dubbo.

Unfortunately, it still hadn't taken her mind off Rachel, completely. She had grilled her relentlessly about Martin when she found out, *after* leaving Trinity, that he was her boyfriend. "Where is he from? What town? What does his father do? Why didn't you tell me about him before?"

And again, there had been a similar reaction when she told her, *after* she had already enrolled at TAFE, that he was attending uni at Canberra. "To think Rachel, you could both be at the same university, and be able to see so much more of each other. If only you had listened to me." She had shaken her head and looked at her with disbelief.

Her parents had finally met Martin on her eighteenth birthday, when he had made the trip from Canberra to spend the weekend with her. Her mother had been a most gracious hostess, while she interrogated him about his family and ambitions for the future. It had come as no surprise to Rachel that on this visit he had chosen to take up Johno's offer, and stay with him instead.

"It's not that I don't appreciate your mother's hospitality Rachel, and you do know that I love knowing you're sleeping in the bedroom next door. I think if I stay with you again though, I might not be able to resist sneaking in to cuddle you while you're fast asleep and dreaming," he had hinted, playing with her hair.

"Hmm, I think it would be a very good idea if you stay with Johno then. You wouldn't want to get on the wrong side of my mother, I can tell you," she had said smiling, although she had actually been relieved that she could blame her mother.

She had no intention of taking their relationship to another level, yet. As much as she loved Martin for his sweetness and thoughtfulness in everything he did for her, she couldn't imagine sharing anything more than their tender kisses and cuddles. Would she eventually feel any different, she wonders, or should she already feel it, after being his girlfriend for over two years? Of course, during most of that time they had still been at boarding school, so they had never had any opportunity for anything else. Yet, now he was suggesting he wanted more. She wonders why she feels nervous about the idea. She isn't entirely naïve, even though she had been closeted away for six years at boarding school. Her mother had quietly handed her the book, "What Every Teenage Girl Should Know," just after she had turned thirteen, but her main sex education had come from the stories of the girls she shared her dormitory with at Trinity, and her recent TAFE friends.

The dream she had last night, has unsettled her too: she was falling, and a man caught her in his arms, carrying her to safety. But, when she had looked into the man's eyes, they weren't the smoky brown of Martin's. They were the colour of a cloudless blue sky.

CHAPTER 14

"Is that what I think it is?" Jess points with the nail polish brush to a book sitting at the back of Rachel's dresser, behind a photo of the two of them in their Trinity uniforms.

Rachel looks up from administering a second coat of lavender nail polish to her neatly manicured nails. "Oh yeah, my old diary. I keep it to remind me of our time together at Trinity."

Jess looks at her with mock seriousness. "Liar," she says without hesitation. "I know who the main subject is, remember, even if I didn't actually read it, like..." Jess falters, wondering if she should have brought the subject up.

"Mandy Morris," Rachel finishes her sentence. "It's ok. I got over it. She never did tell anyone, did she? I ended up feeling a bit sorry for her in the end."

"Never," Jess says sternly.

Rachel smiles at her friend affectionately. "You're such a good friend," she says softly.

Rachel watches Jess studying her newly polished red nails. She's glad she invited her to stay for a few days, and to attend the Dubbo, annual spring Bachelor and Spinsters Ball.

She arrived yesterday afternoon; the smile on her face, as she jumped from the driver's seat and raced over to hug Rachel, as bright as the canary coloured Morris Minor she alighted from. Rachel doesn't think she's smiled, giggled and laughed as much in the last nine months, as she has with Jess, the last twenty-four hours.

"So, where's this B & S thingy being held tonight, and are Martin and Johno picking us up, or are we meeting them there?"

"It's at the showground, and Martin said he'll wait out the front. I was going to drive us in my car, but Dad's offered to drop us off, as long as we catch a taxi home. It's a good idea. We'd probably have trouble finding a park anyway."

"Sounds like it's going to be packed," Jess comments.

Rachel had been looking forward to tonight ever since she knew both Martin and Jess would be coming too, and now, even Johno. That way, there would be four of them, so Jess wouldn't feel like the odd one out.

She's hoping Johno doesn't drink too much tonight. He was a fun person to be around, especially when he'd had a few drinks, but sometimes he'd overdo it and wind up doing things he normally wouldn't.

Like the time he'd taken a garden gnome from the front garden of a house, on his way home from the pub, then put it in the driver's seat of Martin's car. Martin had seen the humour behind the action, as Johno had always called him an old man, and the gnome held a striking resemblance to Martin when he was wearing his glasses for reading. Unfortunately, the old lady who owned the gnome had not seen the humour in it when Martin was caught returning it to her garden the next day. Martin had hardly been fazed by the incident. He said it was only minor compared to some of the stories he could tell her from uni in Canberra. Rachel had wondered about that. Perhaps she was too serious about everything.

"Jess, am I fun to be around?' she asks.

"Of course you are silly. Do you think I'd be here otherwise?"

"Yeah, I guess," she blushes, embarrassed by asking in the first place.

"Well, I think we're going to have a ball tonight at any rate. Ha, ha, cause that's where we're going," Jess says, attempting to cheer her up.

***

The annual Bachelor's and Spinsters Ball, or B & S, as it was commonly known by the younger generations in rural Australia, was traditionally an event hosted in many country towns for young people, eighteen years and over, to find a partner. By 1978, it had evolved into a get-together for friends who often lived great distances from one another. To those living locally it was known as one of the biggest all-night parties of the year; a step up from the live performances conducted at local pubs and clubs, where stricter codes of conduct were enforced.

A charity fund-raiser for the local community, for the cost of the ticket, the youth of the area, far and wide, could consume large amounts of free alcohol and dance to the musical band performing on stage, until their alcohol addled brains took them staggering outside to look for entertainment elsewhere.

This usually culminated in either a riotous bout of 'ute-circling' or a couple sneaking off to find a quiet spot, which sooner or later entailed a lie down in one of the many vehicles parked outside nearby. The next morning both male and female alike would often wake to look across at a face only vaguely remembered from the night before.

The B & S ball couldn't be any more different to the rigorous monitoring of boarding school dances, Rachel was to discover. By now, it was just over nine months since she had left Trinity. She would be nineteen in a few months, and although she had occasionally joined Martin or her TAFE friends at one of the local pubs or clubs for a night out, tonight was to be an eye opener.

It was almost eight o'clock by the time they found Martin

and Johno, although they had been dropped off by her father at seven-thirty. They found them at the bar.

"Hey Rach, Jess," Martin yells above the noise of the band, and Rachel can already taste the beer on his breath as she accepts his quick kiss on the lips. He hands her two white plastic cups of white wine. She passes one to Jess. "Sorry about not waiting out the front. Johno dragged me in here. I figured I'd grab us a drink before it got too packed," he half yells into her ear. She nods and notices Johno throw an empty cup in a bin nearby as he takes a long mouthful of another full one. He smiles at Jess and passes her another cup of white wine, as they try to exchange a few words over the din.

As she sips her wine, Rachel looks around and notices the array of outfits on the people milling past. There's a group of girls her age dressed in long formal dresses, strutting past in their stiletto heels and silk shawls. To her right, a cowboy, donning an Akubra hat, wearing black shiny boots and an R. M. Williams shirt, leans with his back to the wall as he chats with two girls, wearing clothes that could only be found in the antique section of an opportunity shop, or their grandmother's closets. To her left, several other girls are dressed similar to herself, in fashionable jeans and shirts. She's now glad she wore the new emerald green silk shirt she bought at 'Suzanne' in the arcade, yesterday. She thought it looked good with her dark blue denim jeans and side-zip black boots. It seems Martin thinks so too, because she notices him appraising her and when she questions him with raised eyebrows, he caresses her back and mouths, "Wow."

All of a sudden Jess grabs her by the arm and drags her onto the dance floor. Martin shrugs with a grin and turns to join Johno at the bar.

After several dances Rachel's finding it hard to breathe, being hemmed in by all the people around her, and she's still not sure if that man dancing close by was deliberately brushing himself up against her or not. She gestures to Jess that she needs to go outside to cool down, and Jess follows. She looks for Martin in the area of the bar, as she leaves, but realises it would take too long to push through the crowd to find him. She needs fresh air, now!

The night air hits her face as they find their way outside and she sighs in relief. The September breeze is blowing gently, and she understands now why the B & S Ball is held in spring. There are people milling about everywhere, and all the seats near the entrance are filled. Two men suddenly appear beside them.

"Hello beautiful," one of the men says, and leers at Rachel, while his friend moves over closer to Jess, drains the remainder of his drink and belches. "Wanna have a good time?" the man beside Rachel says, winking, and sidling up to her, rubbing his hand across her backside before she can respond.

"Bugger off." She pushes his arm away, grabs Jess by the hand and walks quickly away. She scans the perimeter and spots a wooden bench under a tree some distance away, pulling Jess to it. Although it's out of the lightened area, it was worth the short walk she decides as they sit down and rest their legs.

"I guess it's open slather here tonight," Jess sighs, and opens the tiny leather shoulder bag nestled in her lap. She pulls out her compact mirror and lipstick and commences to apply it. "You'd better check this for me before we go back inside. I can't really see where it's going," she says, giggling.

Although there isn't much light where they are sitting, Rachel is aware Jess's comment has nothing to do with that. She remembers she had downed two glasses of white wine just before they had hit the dance floor.

"Did you see Martin or Johno anywhere while we were dancing," she asks her.

"Hmm, yeah, I think they were at the bar, but Martin didn't look too happy."

"Yes, well, I guess he's keeping an eye on Johno," she concludes.

"Aww, don't worry girlfriend. I'm here." Jess affectionately bumps her with her shoulder, and begins to put her compact mirror and lipstick away.

Rachel smiles, glad that her friend *is* in fact, with her. She doesn't think she would be enjoying herself otherwise.

"Well, I guess we should try to find them though, in case Martin starts to wonder where we are. You right?" Rachel asks, and assuming she is, she stands and starts to walk back to the door as Jess is still trying to latch her bag on her lap.

All of a sudden the loud roar of an engine starts up and a vehicle comes hurtling towards Rachel. The next minute, she hears Jess scream her name, as a man comes charging out of no-where like a bull, scoops her up over his shoulder and runs. She doesn't know what is happening, although she's aware there's a strong man carrying her because his shoulder feels like a rock against her stomach. She hears voices yelling and the screech of a vehicle pulling up, and she thinks she must be winded because she can't catch her breath, let alone speak. Then, her assailant's strong arms lift her from his shoulder and gently lay her on a soft grassy mound, and she looks up, into the eyes of Darel, and faints.

Rachel's not sure how long she was unconscious, but when she opens her eyes, Jess is cradling her head in her lap and Martin is kneeling beside her, holding her hand. "Thank God. Are you ok Rachel?" Martin grips her hand tighter.

"Yes, I think so. What happened?" she asks, although she knows Darel had carried her to where she now lay. She looks around earnestly for him.

"Some idiot decided to do some circling."

Rachel frowns at Martin, confused.

"It's a ute club competition. Johno told me about it. It's where they drive their utes in as small a circle as possible, at the fastest possible speed," he explains. "He said he didn't see you, but I know for sure he'd have trouble seeing anything now, even if he had, after the punch that bloke gave him in the eye."

"What bloke?" Rachel asks, breathlessly.

Martin looks around, and points to a couple walking away toward the front gate of the show ground. "*That* bloke. Do you know him Rachel?" Martin asks as he helps her stand up. "He's the one that saved you," he says softly, not waiting for a reply, and stands directly in front of her. "It should have been *me*, and I should have been with you. I'm so sorry Rachel," he whispers, and holds her tight against him.

Rachel's head is swirling. She wants to look over his shoulder at Darel, but she had noticed he was walking away with a woman by his side, when Martin had pointed to him. She can't bear to see if he's holding her hand. She just wants to get away from where she is right now. "I want to go home Martin," she says softly.

"I'd drive you home Rachel, but Johno and I walked here from his place. I'll have to go call a taxi from the servo. Ok?"

Johno and Jess stay with Rachel, while Martin jogs to the service station, about a block away, to call a taxi.

She had planned on getting a taxi home, with Jess, anyway, at the end of the Ball. But, after what has just happened, she hopes Martin won't now insist on going with her.

She also doesn't want her parents to know what has happened, and she knows they would be curious if Martin turned up with her, when she had already told them he was staying with Johno.

Jess has just told her that she is going home with her now, whether she likes it or not. Rachel is pleased about that, because now she can tell Martin that he should stay and keep Johno company.

She's told herself that these are the reasons she doesn't want him to escort her home, but somehow the truth keeps niggling her; she just doesn't want to be with him while she has Darel on her mind. And, she feels guilty.

So, when the taxi arrives shortly after he returned, Rachel is relieved she's able to convince him to stay, adding, "I'll be fine. Thank you. Ring me tomorrow."

CHAPTER 15

Rachel watches Jess leaning against the verandah railing, looking at the stars.

"I'm sorry we had to come home early."

Jess turns to look at her and smiles gently, "Hey, no problem." She studies Rachel thoughtfully. "I think you know who that hunk was though."

Caught off guard, Rachel doesn't answer, and Jess grins. "Aha, I knew you did. Tell me, tell me..."

Jess is Rachel's best girlfriend. She knows her well enough to know she'll keep a secret. Just like she did with Darel, before, she remembers. She won't be able to think about anything else now, so she might as well share her thoughts; well, at least *some* of them.

"It was Darel," Rachel almost whispers, looking to see if the window is closed to the lounge room where her parents are still watching television.

"Oh Rachel. You lucky thing," Jess croons. "You have Martin and your old knight in shining armour too."

"Yeah sure, as if," she replies, but noticing the surprised look on Jess's face she continues, "...of course I have Martin, and I know he's great and all, but Darel was just being...Darel." She looks down at her hands.

"Hmmm, so Darel just goes around rescuing *anyone* who is in trouble then," Jess says sarcastically, with raised eyebrows.

"I guess, probably. Well, I wouldn't put it past him," she tries to back up her previous statement.

Jess looks at Rachel and shakes her head. "It seems to me girlfriend, you need to have a good long think about it."

"What's there to think about?" she retorts. "Didn't you see him walking away with that woman? Why would it make any difference what I think?"

"Ok, ok, don't get your nickers in a knot. It was just weird the way he was the only one who noticed that ute in the dark. He must have been watching you very closely, that's all," Jess says quietly as she looks at Rachel for a while, before returning her gaze to the heavens.

***

"Rachel, Martin's on the phone," her mother yells as she opens the gauze door to the back garden where Rachel and Jess are lying on beach towels soaking up the sun.

"About time," she mutters, as she stands up and walks quickly into the house.

It was almost lunch-time, but she wasn't all that surprised the boys had partied on after she and Jess had left.

It had been a Saturday night, as well as the B & S Ball. There would be plenty of sore heads this morning in Dubbo, she imagines.

"Hi Martin," she says brightly, into the phone. "How's your head?" She adds with a chuckle.

"Morning, beautiful. Ahhh, not too bad." He replies sheepishly.

"So what's the plan for today?"

"Recovery. Johno and I are at The Railway. Wanna drag Jess along for a counter lunch and a game of pool?"

"I guess, if Jess wants to," Rachel concedes, although she would much rather go to park by the river for a picnic lunch. She enjoyed sitting on the grass and feeding the ducks there with left-over bread. Over the last few weeks she had noticed some baby ducklings too. It was relaxing, to watch the little family swimming in the water, or waddling over the grass.

"Come on gorgeous, it won't be the same without you. I didn't get to see much of you last night remember, and I'm leaving early tomorrow morning."

"How could I say 'no', to that," she says smiling, feeling touched by his words. Besides, she knows Jess will be all for it, thinking how Jess's night out had been shortened last night as well. "We'll see you soon."

***

Jess follows Rachel into the main bar area of the Railway

Hotel, and around the corner to the pool table area. At that moment, Martin pots the black ball into the end pocket of the pool table he and Johno are playing on, winning the game.

"Perfect timing," he says, placing his pool cue onto the table as Rachel comes closer and plants a quick kiss on his lips.

Johno places his pool cue beside Martin's and puckers his lips comically while walking towards Jess with a cheeky grin, but she slaps him playfully.

"Ok, lets eat," Martin says, guiding them all back into the main bar, through a door and along a hallway to the beer garden at the back of the Hotel.

A few minutes later, as they wait for their orders, Martin retreats back into the bar for a round of drinks, returning soon after with two schooners of beer, and two glasses of apple cider for the girls.

"So, what happened at the B & S after we left last night," Jess asks, looking at Martin and Johno, expectantly.

"Not much," Johno replies.

When Martin doesn't add anything, Jess smirks. "Well, aren't you two a source of information then?"

Martin complies. "Well, we stayed till about midnight, but by then it was getting pretty full-on, so we called it a night."

"What do you mean, full-on, what happened?" Jess asks, wondering if any more dramas had unfolded.

"Aww, nothin' much. Just lots of drinkin' and foolin' around," Johno tries to dismiss it, looking at Rachel.

Rachel doesn't want to discuss last night, unlike Jess, and although Johno seems happy to drop it, Martin is now thinking about it. He reaches over and places his hand over Rachel's, resting on the table.

"Did he hurt you?"

Rachel looks at him, confused.

"When he threw you over his shoulder," he says, reminding her.

"He didn't *throw* me," she snaps, and then realises her error. "No, I'm fine Martin. I just got a bit winded, that's all.

Jess and Johno are both watching the discussion, but then turn to look at one another and smile, knowingly.

Johno is now convinced that Jess also knows it was Darel Rutherford who prevented Rachel from being run over by a ute last night.

Johno was born in Dubbo, and once he returned home from St Michael's, the boy's equivalent of the girl's, Trinity, in Orange, he started work at his father's car dealership. He also attends TAFE as part of his mechanics apprenticeship his father insisted on. He has been friends with Martin since St Michael's, and so he knows about as much as Martin does about Jess, but now discovers, even more than he does, about Rachel. He often bumps into Rachel at TAFE, and part of his job at work is to assist the more experienced mechanics service the vehicles brought in from customers in the area; one of the most recent customer's, being, Darel Rutherford.

So, although both he and Martin had seen Darel running across the grassy area at the front of the building with Rachel over his shoulder last night, from behind the throng of people at the door, *he* had recognised Darel straight away.

He had also walked in to the office at work one day, and overheard his father explaining about the Rutherford account to their administration assistant. "Work carried out for both Don and Darel Rutherford is to go on the same account, with the invoice posted to Jannali, even though Darel now lives at the Winton place, next door." It wasn't rocket science to work out that Rachel had once lived next door to him.

He's now very curious as to why she hasn't mentioned it, and by the look on Jess's face, it seems this is something Martin doesn't know about. So, why all the secrecy, he wonders.

Although his loyalty should be to his mate, Martin, and he could come straight out and get to the bottom of it, he's feeling he should sit on the fence. Rachel is his friend too, and if truth be known, he's spent more time with her at TAFE, during breaks and lunch, than he has with Martin since they'd all left school. He's got a lot of time for Rachel. She's looking very uncomfortable at the moment, so he attempts to change the subject.

"Hey Rachel, how's the Corolla going? Probably due for a service by now, don't ya think?

"Yeah, I think you're right. I'll check my book," she says brightly, grateful for the change of subject. It was good having a mechanic as a friend, even if he was still training. The second hand white Corolla her parents gave her for her eighteenth birthday had been the best birthday present, *ever*. Johno has just reminded her of something she wanted to ask him. "I've been meaning to ask you about a clicking noise I sometimes hear when I'm driving."

"Is it coming from the engine?"

"Yeah, I think so. It's probably nothing," she says, waving her hand to dismiss it.

"I'll get the guys at the garage to have a look when you bring it in for a service. Ok?" As she nods her head, he adds, "Soon?" She nods again.

While they have been discussing her car, Martin and Jess have been deep in discussion about uni. They both attend the Australian National University in Canberra, but so far haven't crossed paths there yet. Rachel and Johno now listen to their conversation, as they all eat their meals.

"Yeah, Deakin Street is the best," Jess says conclusively,

while planting her fork into her last piece of steak, dripping with gravy.

"The best what?" Rachel asks.

"Chinese restaurant," both Martin and Jess say in unison, and then laugh together.

"Is that the one where you work part-time at night," Rachel asks.

"Yes, of course. That's why it's the best," Jess answers, giggling.

"I didn't know you liked Chinese food, Martin," Rachel comments.

"Well, now you do," he says with a grin.

"You should go try it out. Where Jess works." Rachel suggests. Jess and Martin both look at her, and then at each other. "Well then you can tell me what you think, Martin," she continues. "Maybe I'll come visit you both at uni sometime, now I have wheels. We can go give Jess a hard time," she says cheekily.

"Come to think of it," Martin jumps in. "Jess, if we're ever both coming to Dubbo at the same time again, maybe we could share. You know, you go with me, I go with you. Save petrol."

Jess looks at Rachel, trying to gauge her reaction.

Rachel shrugs. "Sounds like a good idea," she says, as she lifts her fork to her mouth, with the last piece of bream from her plate, remembering how Darel's favourite food was also fish, caught in the river at Janalli.

They spend the next few hours playing pool against each other in pairs, and although she's pleased to see Martin and Johno ease up on their drinking, Rachel notes the conversation increases; especially between Martin and Jess.

It isn't that she minds. She is still battling internally with her thoughts, which are at loggerheads with her emotions, and finding it difficult to concentrate on conversation anyway. She is pleased her boyfriend and girlfriend get on well. But, she is starting to get annoyed with herself for not being able to relax more, hitting the pool balls in frustration, and even knocking a few of them onto the floor.

"Do you play tennis Rachel?" Johno asks.

"Not since Trinity." She notices him considering something. "Why?"

"Well, I'm gunno go in the night comp. But, I need a female partner. The way you're bashin' those balls, I reckon we could do well together," he says grinning.

Rachel rolls her eyes. "Ha, ha, very funny."

"No, I'm serious. Wanna play?"

Rachel thinks it would probably be fun. She makes an instant decision. "Yeah, why not."

"Ok, cool. I'll put your name down. Thanks." He needs a partner for the comp, but he's also remembered seeing Darel

Rutherford's name on the list. One way to get to the bottom of this, he thinks.

Later, they all go back to Johno's flat, after stopping by the video shop to rent some movies. The boys had quickly grabbed, 'Jaws' and 'Halloween', but the girls insisted on "Grease"; their reasoning being, that it had only just been released and it starred an Aussie, Olivia Newton-John.

"You gotta support home-grown talent," Jess admonishes the boys.

"Well, we have sharks in Australia too, you know," Johno had smartly commented, referring to his choice of, 'Jaws'.

A compromise was made, after the girls also found, 'The Rocky Horror Picture Show'. They decided they would all watch, 'Jaws' and 'The Rocky Horror Picture Show', at Johno's flat, together, and then the girls could take 'Grease' back to her parents place, while the boys watched 'Halloween'.

Martin and Rachel had snuggled up together on the three-seater lounge, after Johno had thrown a rug over it to cover up the grease marks left from his work clothes. Johno hadn't needed to claim *his* chair, a second hand recliner bought from a mate, who had recently upgraded to a flash new one. It was quite evident from the empty beer cans beside it that it was the most used chair. Jess had plopped into the dark brown bean bag as if she were a regular visitor.

By the time the second movie had finished the sun was beginning to set. Rachel and Jess decided it was time to go. The boys had both nodded off during 'The Rocky Horror Picture Show', much to the girl's amusement, especially as the volume was up high.

"I bet they get their second wind though," Jess says as they drive back to her parents place.

"Yeah, I can't imagine them sleeping through 'Halloween'.

"Can't wait to watch 'Grease', John Travolta is so dreamy looking," Jess drools.

Rachel smiles at her friend. She was looking forward to watching it also. It would be even better watching it alone with her girlfriend. They could talk while it was on, unlike the boys, who constantly ignored their comments and frowned at them to be quiet.

Later that night, Rachel and Jess are lying in their beds in her room, when Jess asks.

"You didn't mind Martin suggesting we drive together to see you, did you?"

"No, of course not. Why should I worry about that?" she asks in all seriousness.

"Yeah, I know. I mean, it's not like you have anything to worry about, or anything. Between Martin and me, I mean."

"Hmm," Rachel agrees, drifting off to sleep.

"Hey Rach, are you going to go see Darel, and thank him?"

Rachel's eyes open wide, and she is glad that Jess can't see her in the dark. "Maybe," she says.

"Well, I know *I* would," Jess states, and bites her tongue, glad that Rachel can't see her face in the dark, either. Sometimes her friend needs a little pushing, but she has to pick the right moments.

"Yes, well, I've been thinking about it. Night," she says, not wanting the conversation to continue, and turns away from Jess. And yet, try as she might, to return to her earlier state of pre-sleep, she tossed and turned for another half hour before finally falling asleep, dreaming of the river overflowing at Binda.

CHAPTER 16

By the beginning of October, Rachel still hadn't seen Darel. It had been over a month since the B & S Ball and Martin and Jess had gone back to Canberra.

It had been busy at work, filling seed orders, fencing materials and dispensing a myriad of supplies. But, although every afternoon she hoped Darel might turn up at work like he had before, come closing time, she would say goodbye to the other staff, and dejectedly walk to her car.

She had picked up the phone at home to ring him, about two weeks ago, when her parents hadn't been around, but she thought it would look strange by then, having taken so long to call. She chided herself; it would have been polite to have at least done that a few days after the B & S. But, the thought of hearing his voice at the other end of the line, and knowing he would be able to read her thoughts from her voice, deterred her. Then there was also the possibility that that other woman might be there. The thought that she might be listening to their conversation had soon put an end to the idea of speaking to him over the phone.

Her secretarial studies at TAFE had also kept her largely

occupied, with only a few months until the end of the year, and the final examinations around the corner. She wasn't concerned about gaining her credentials, because she had been able to put the majority of the theory she had learned to practical use at work. Experience was always the best teacher, she reminded herself. But, despite applying herself conscientiously to her studies and work, she still couldn't keep thoughts of Darel far from her mind.

So, when Johno reminded her at TAFE, that the tennis comp was starting the following Friday, she was very glad. It would be a good distraction, and probably what she needed; some fun.

When she pulled up at the town tennis courts, and looked towards the club house, she had been surprised to see so many familiar faces. Several of her TAFE friends were there, as well as some familiar faces from Barwon. There were both male and female participants from all ages.

The courts weren't new to her. When she had been in primary school, her parents had often played in the Dubbo tennis competitions. At those times, however, she had had to either watch the adults playing or find some other way to kill the time. She had always had a book to resort to, when she wasn't practising her forehand on the practice brick wall at the side of the courts. She remembers her mother saying that she had met her father at a social tennis competition. *Thank goodness Mum now plays lawn bowls instead of tennis*, she thinks.

She spots Johno walking quickly towards her as she exits her car.

"Hey," he says. "Looks like we're on straight up. You'd better go pay inside so we can get the ball rolling, or over the net at least." He smiles and pulls a face at his own quip.

Rachel chuckles at his attempt at humour, regardless, and walks quickly towards the club house.

It took a few games to warm up again, but once she and Johno had worked out how the other played, they soon melded well into a successful partnership.

Johno liked to play on the baseline, preferring to slug it out with long volleys. Rachel, on the other hand, was more than adept at strategically intercepting and diverting the balls at the net. As they walked off the court, from their first win of the night, Rachel found she was enjoying herself immensely. They both sat down on the wooden tennis bench where they had left their tennis racquet covers and backpacks. Johno pulled out a water bottle and commenced to drink.

"I knew I'd forgotten something," Rachel said. She rummages through her backpack and finds her purse. "They still have the drink machine inside?" she asks Johno.

"Yeah, about half way, to the right."

Rachel nods and walks inside the club house to the drink

machine. She chooses bottled water, and then bends down to collect her drink from the slot at the bottom of the machine and the change from the coin dispensary. As she stands up, she turns, and nearly runs into Darel, standing in front of her.

"Hi Rach."

"Oh, hi Darel." She straight away knows what to say next. "I've been wanting to thank you....for helping me at the B & S Ball. I'm sorry I didn't ring you, but I thought I might see you at work....like I did before." She waits for him to answer. *Why is he looking at me that way?*

"No problem Rach. Never was, never will be." He says softly. "I just can't help but...well, let's just say, old habits die hard." He looks past her briefly, as if distracted by something. She then realises, it's *someone*, as he motions with his hand, requesting whoever it is to join him. He continues, "I've been in a few times since the B & S...but you weren't there."

Curious, Rachel turns to look in the direction he had been looking, and immediately recognises the woman she had seen him leaving with the night of the B & S Ball. She has to get away, and right *now*.

"Oh ok, never mind. Well, I'm glad I was able to see you here. I had better..." she starts to say, about to walk off quickly, when Darel interrupts her.

"Rach, I just want you to meet…"

"I really better get back outside," she says, interrupting him. "I think I'm on soon. Maybe some other time. Bye." She races away just as the woman walks up to Darel.

When she arrives back to where she had last seen Johno, she asks straight away, "When are we on next?"

Johno has been watching Court 4, knowing it was where they were to play their next match. "Right now Rach," he says, noticing the four players starting to walk towards the tennis court gate.

Rachel gulps down some of her water, picks up her racquet and follows Johno onto the tennis courts. Their opponents are close behind them, and they all walk along the side of the tennis fence to Court 4.

As they all reach the net, Johno introduces himself to their opponents. Rachel introduces herself too, although Johno is surprised at her abruptness. She seems preoccupied. He then notices her look back at the club house a few times, as if she is searching for someone. If he were to hazard a guess, he thinks she may have noticed her former neighbour somewhere in the last few minutes. He had noticed him walk into the club house shortly after Rachel had. The last time he had seen that look on her face had been at the B & S Ball, after the ute incident, when Martin had pointed to Darel leaving.

"You ok Rachel? he asks, as they walk to take their places, after tossing to see who will serve first.

"Um, yeah. Fine, fine," she stammers, before taking a big breath and expelling it.

The match kicks off with both Rachel and Johno both unfocussed. While for Rachel, it had been because she had noticed Darel and the other woman walking on to Court 2, for Johno it had a lot to do with the female opponent on the other side of the net.

On the up side, Johno's flirting relaxed Rachel, which made her uncharacteristically less harsh on her own poor performance. Where normally she would have been chastising herself for missing a ball speeding past her, she now just mouthed, 'sorry' to Johno, and waited for the next one.

When Johno held the game up with his funny antics in an attempt to gain the attention of the cute brunette on the other side of the court, Rachel was able to sneak a look at Darel, two courts away.

He was certainly a good player, she noted, and she could easily understand why he had earned the nickname, Ace. She wondered if he was still called it, or whether it had just been while he had been at High School. She watched him serve to both his male and female opponents, while collecting the balls in between her own game. While he aced the male opponent nearly every time, he served much more softly to the female. He would give the female opponent the opportunity to return the ball. She imagines playing as his partner. She knows she would enjoy it.

She then looks at his partner, properly, for the first time, and something tugs at her memory. She is almost the same height as Darel, quite tall for a woman; *a few centimetres taller than me,* she thinks. She is slender with an almost boyish figure, but still feminine with her moderate sized breasts and shapely buttocks and legs. *Hmm, I'm a bit curvier than she is,* she decides, comparing herself. There isn't really anything overall, that rings any bells, but when she looks more closely at her face she's now convinced, she's seen her before, somewhere. But, *where?*

Somehow, Rachel and Johno finished their match, still in one piece, along with an unsurprising loss. She almost wondered if she would need to call an ambulance right at the end of the match though, when Johno had tried to jump over the net to congratulate the winners, and tripped, landing on his head. If she didn't know Johno as well as she did, she may have even considered it had been deliberate, judging by the concern and sympathy it generated from the female opponent. He had staggered off the tennis courts with an arm over the shoulders of both girls, but when he had turned sideways and grinned at Rachel, she had rolled her eyes, removed his arm from her shoulder and left him to the other girl's attentions.

Darel and his partner left before Rachel and Johno had been half way through their second and last match for the night. She had watched the competitors shaking hands as she was preparing to serve. Darel had glanced over and waved at her just at that moment. She had waved back, and surprised herself by then acing her male opponent, her first ace for the night. She had looked back to him to see if he had noticed, but he had been walking towards the court gate with his back to her. She chanced another look after her next serve and volley, and saw them turning together at the corner of the club house toward the car park.

After she leaves Johno, she walks briskly to her car and within seconds she's driving out of the tennis club car park. She decides to take the long way home, where the road runs parallel to the river. After a few minutes, the river comes into view to the side of the road, and on impulse, she pulls into the car park she has visited many times since owning her own car.

She turns off the car lights and ignition. It's a bright night. She can see all around her and even across to the bank on the other side of the river. The water is sparkling in the moonlight and she gets out of her car, and walks over to sit on a grassy knoll close to the riverbank. She looks up to the source of the light, a glorious full moon, and at the stars; the

Southern Cross. It takes her breath away, the beauty of it all.

When they were younger, Darel told her that his mother's people called the Southern Cross, star constellation, 'Mirrabooka'. He told her the dreaming story: *Mirrabooka was once a kind and wise man who looked after his people so well that the Creator Spirit, 'Biyaami', decided to reward him by granting him eternal life once he died on earth. When that day came, Biyammi placed him in the sky and stretched him across it.* Darel had said, the white man call Mirrabooka, the Southern Cross, and the two most prominent stars, the Pointers, or Alpha and Beta Centauri. But, his mother said they are really Mirrabooka's eyes — watching over the earth.

Rachel finds comfort in the scene above her; majestic, immovable, yet at the same time, gentle and soothing. She imagines people from all around the world looking at the very same image; in loud joyful appreciation, or silent awe of the grandeur of it all; even for solace. Perhaps they were seeking guidance, like she now was.

"What should I do?" she entreats out loud.

She thinks about the teachings of both Christianity and aborigine Spirituality, in caring and treating each other with respect and kindness. That was one thing she has always tried to do, but comes to the conclusion, she has so far, failed.

She hasn't been kind to Martin. She hasn't treated him the way he treats her. She can't imagine him thinking about another woman when he is with her; like she thinks of Darel when she's with him. She cringes at the thought. If Martin were able to read her thoughts, he would certainly feel betrayed.

She thinks about how their relationship had started. She remembers the night she had first encouraged him, and she groans. She had been trying to put Darel out of her mind. She had even been thinking about Darel the first time he had kissed her, and if she were entirely honest with herself, she has been doing it ever since.

And yet, he loves her and wants to be with her, despite the inconvenience of the distance between them. It isn't the most ideal relationship, being so far apart from each other by distance. And, as a uni student, he needed to be careful with his finances. Even calling her every week, and putting petrol in the tank of his Fiat, took a great deal from his limited funds. But then it hits her; she hasn't heard from him since the B & S Ball, over a month ago now. Why hadn't she even noticed before now?

Everything had seemed as normal when he had left, but had he somehow known more than she thought? Or, had he started to question their relationship too? He had hinted he wanted their relationship to move to another level, and she had made it clear that she didn't. So, where were they heading anyway? It wasn't as if she had any plans about leaving Dubbo, and he was going to be at uni in Canberra for a few more years yet. She really should have been thinking more seriously about her relationship with Martin.

As for Darel, well, she will just have to *make* herself stop thinking about him. What is *wrong* with me? she admonishes herself. He has a woman in his life now, and even if it is the hardest thing she has ever had to do, she *must* stop thinking about him. She admits, she loves him. But is it because he is so much a part of Binda, she can't separate him from it? Could it be, that because she *can't* have either Binda or Darel, she wants them both so much? Is it, that she only *think*s she loves him? She shakes her head, debating with herself, but then thinks of one of her favourite quotes: *'If you love something, set it free. If it comes back to you, it's yours. If it doesn't, it never really was.'* Well, that pretty much sums it up, she admits, and wraps her arms around herself for comfort, when the arrows of truth pierce her heart.

Martin loves her, or at least, he did. She thinks she loves Darel, but he will never be hers now, anyway. She decides she must stop allowing her heart to interfere with the truth that is staring her in the face. And when she looks at it squarely, she realises she must make a decision and see it through.

Tomorrow she will go to Binda, one last time, to say a final 'goodbye' to both Binda and Darel. She'll then go to Canberra the following weekend to see Martin and work out if they should continue their relationship. She has to start thinking about what is best for everyone, not just for herself; honour her conscious. Otherwise, she'll never find peace.

She might need some time with her best girlfriend after that, to cheer her up. She decides to ring Jess when she gets back from Binda and let her know she's coming to visit.

Satisfied with her plans, she looks up to the sky once more and whispers, 'thank you', from her heart.

CHAPTER 17

Rachel touches the brake gently with her foot as she approaches the village of Barwon. She's travelled for almost fifty minutes since leaving Dubbo, but the time has seemed to fly by. Memories and inner conversation have occupied her mind the entire distance.

She is expecting Darel to be at Binda, even though it's Saturday afternoon. She had imagined the only reason he wouldn't be at Binda today would be if he were playing in a cricket match, either at Barwon or Dubbo. But she knows cricket season hasn't kicked off yet, because she asked her father this morning. And Darel played tennis last night, so unless he has other plans, there's a good chance he'll be there. She doesn't want to have to make this trip again. It would be too hard. *Yes, I should have rung first.* But what would she have said? "Hi Darel, I just want to come out and say goodbye?" No, she can't see that making much sense.

Despite waking late this morning and feeling haunted by a dream refusing to leave the fringes of her mind, she had still been determined to carry out her plan. She had sat outside in the sunshine, drinking her hot milo, watching her mother weed the garden, and listening to the voices and laughter of the children next door as they jumped on their trampoline. She had almost started to feel sleepy again from the warmth of the sun, until she saw her father duck inside the garden shed and return with the lawnmower. She had then quickly retreated to the quietness of the house. Once she had her washing on the clothesline, flapping gaily in the breeze, she had eaten a quick lunch while chatting amicably with her father. She had then announced, "I'm going for a drive. See you later," and headed quickly out the door before she could change her mind, or either of her parents had asked her where she was going.

At first it had felt strange, concentrating on driving on the road to Binda. It was the first time she had driven this way herself. Before she had her own car, as a passenger and a young girl, her eyes had been able to wander freely, as she had gazed out the window at the endless paddocks of wheat, oats, barley, and the sheep grazing on the grasslands. The motion of the car had often lulled her into a dream-like state, allowing her mind to drift away to wherever her imagination had taken her.

On the nights they had travelled home from tennis competitions her parents had participated in, she had watched transfixed as the setting sun slowly melted behind the hills, amidst a kaleidoscope of colour. And still other nights, when the land was in darkness and startled rabbits and kangaroos scurried away from the approaching headlights of the car, she would look up at the moon staring down at her, until her eyes closed to dream. Thinking about that, reminds her of her dream last night.

She had been standing, facing Darel beside the river at Binda. He had been pointing to something behind her, but she had been distracted by two people standing behind him. When she looked at their faces, she saw the woman Darel had been with at the B and S Ball and tennis last night, and Darel's mother. The dream had ended there.

She tries to decipher it. She could relate to being by the river with Darel. It had, after all, been their favourite meeting place, and when she thinks of Darel she often thinks of being there together. She wonders what he had been pointing at though. She had been standing, facing him with the river to her left, and to his right, so he had been pointing in the direction of the dividing fence. Why would he be pointing there? Jannali was on the other side of the fence, and she already knew that. But when she thinks about it more, it seems he could have been pointing to something, *at* the fence. As she's not able to think of anything but the fence and the big white gum tree, she gives up and moves on to the faces of the woman and his mother. They hadn't been looking at her. They had been more like projections from

Darel; just there, in the background. She feels sad thinking about it, because she now believes her dream was telling her that just as his mother is part of him, his life, now that other woman is also. Well, that was probably why she hadn't wanted to think about it this morning. It was just confirmation that she needed to let go, she decides.

Her attention is brought back to the present by the tapping noise she hears coming from the front of the car. It seems to be much louder now she's driving faster. Johno had advised her to get it checked, she remembers. She decides she'd better book it in next week.

She tries to ignore it, and as she drives on she envisages all the familiar things she will soon see; the pothole that's always needed repairing in the bitumen near the Barwon Public School, the white skeletal tree looking like an old bent man by the roadside just after the turn-off to Wilson's Lane, and the old weather beaten shed at the half-way point between Barwon and Binda. This feeling of knowing and belonging is unsettling. Like Binda and Darel, it seems like everything is etched in her mind and heart, forever.

The Corolla slowly stops at the front gate of Binda as her foot grinds the brake pedal to the floor. *I could turn around right now, and he'll never know I came*, she thinks, trembling slightly with trepidation. *Coward!*, she admonishes herself. *You know you have to do this Rachel*, she retaliates in an internal struggle. Her stomach churns.

Gingerly, she takes her foot off the brake, and places it onto the accelerator, driving slowly through the open gate. *Binda, always so welcoming. It's nice to see at least that hasn't changed.* The thought propels her forward, along the stretch of front driveway lined with poplar trees, in anticipation of seeing her old home.

As she nears the house, she hears dogs barking through her open window. She stares at the overgrown white miniature rose-hedge protecting the house it surrounds. *It's grown so much, and looks so beautiful*, she thinks nostalgically. Any minute now she'll see either a woman or Darel, walk into view. She takes a deep breath. Although she expects it will be the woman, she prays silently that she will be spared. The last time she was here, her mother was the woman of the house. She doesn't think she can bear being invited inside to see it now, void of anything familiar. That is, of course, *if* she's invited in. It only just occurs to her that her presence may not be welcomed. Yet, although conversation has seemed awkward between them when they've met in town, she's still on friendly terms with Darel, and the former owner's daughter of Binda. Surely, that accounts for something.

The barks of the dogs are winding down, but she has no intention of getting out of the car until someone appears. She turns off the engine and notices a black and white border collie walking back and forth in front of the car, and through the rear vision mirror, a kelpie of a deep tan colour, at the back. She doesn't recognise them. *They must be Darel's.* She remembers her father saying now that his dogs went to another farm in the district. *It looks like these dogs have rounded me up...waiting for instruction from their owners. I'm trapped.*

Once more, she's starting to consider leaving before anyone sees her, when the shadow of a figure appears beside her. She jumps in her seat.

"Hello?" The woman stands beside her door, and her hazel coloured eyes look inquiringly at Rachel. *Where have I seen those eyes before? Rachel wonders.*

"Oh, hello." Rachel tries to smile as she composes herself and fumbles out of the car, causing the woman to step backwards. Rachel thinks she must be waiting for her to introduce herself.

"Um, I'm Rachel, and..."

"Yes, I know who you are Rachel," the woman interrupts, looking slightly amused.

"Oh, ok. And your name is...?

"Grace," I'm Darel's ...

"I hope you don't mind, but I was wondering if I could have a few words with Darel if he's around." Rachel interrupts, before Grace can finish her sentence.

A small smile plays at Grace's lips, and her head rolls to

one side as she studies Rachel's face. "Well, he's doing some fencing down at the dividing fence. You'd know, the one between Jannali and here, by the river. I was just about to take him some smoko, but...you can take it to him if you'd like to? Grace waits expectantly.

Rachel sighs with relief, although slightly confused at the request. Why would she so willingly encourage her to be with Darel, alone? However, it dawns on her that there wouldn't be any reason for Grace to be unfriendly towards her. Obviously, Darel's mentioned her as his childhood friend. Rachel pulls herself together.

"Yes, no problem. I don't want to interrupt him working, just a quick word or two. That's all."

"Ok, I'll be back in a minute." Grace turns towards the house, but stops and turns back. "Would you like to come in?"

"No! Um, no thank you. I'll wait here." Rachel tries to smile.

A few minutes later Rachel pulls up beside a copse by the river, alongside a motor bike. She looks over towards the dividing fence and notices he has been repairing it; the fencing wire and tools scattered close by Darel's ute, where a portion of the fence is missing. He wouldn't be far away. She takes the esky and thermos from the seat beside her and walks towards the river.

As she comes into the clearing, she looks down and Darel is squatting by the river bank, splashing his face with water. The shirt on his back strains against well-toned muscles as he reaches forward to cup the water from the river into his hands. It is evident that living on the land has made him strong and resilient. As she walks with shaky legs toward him, a dry twig snaps underfoot.

"You've lost your touch Rach," he says casually, still facing the water.

"I see you haven't," she counters.

He stands and turns to her. "I'm not so sure about that, these days," he says more seriously now, looking squarely into her eyes.

Rachel's heart starts to hammer as she looks back into his eyes. She must remember why she's here. She motions to the esky and thermos in her hands. "Grace asked me to bring these to you. Here you go," she says, holding them forward for him to take.

They sit side by side in silence, on the log overlooking the river, as Darel pours the tea. There are two mugs, she notices. The second one would have been meant for Grace, no doubt. She turns her attention to her surroundings.

"It hasn't changed, has it?" Rachel says, a few moments later, as she gazes adoringly along the river bank.

"No, the land doesn't change. It's people that change,"

he says disdainfully.

"Hmm, sometimes people don't have a choice."

"There's always a choice."

Rachel tries to bite her tongue, but his words hit her hard, and she can't help but retaliate. "How can you say that, when you know my choice to stay at Binda was taken from me? And have you forgotten about your mother? Where was *her* choice?

Darel suddenly stands and tips the contents of his mug onto the ground, and glares at Rachel. "Why are you here Rachel?" he asks vehemently.

Rachel grimaces. She should have known better than to have mentioned his mother. How could she have been so thoughtless? Well, perhaps his anger will make what she has to say, easier.

"I'm here to say a final goodbye, to...Binda," she says with a tremble in her voice.

"Well, I should have seen that comin'." He says bitterly.

Rachel thinks Darel's still upset by her comment about his mother. She doesn't trust herself to speak right now, because she doesn't want to hurt him any further, and yet her emotions are playing havoc with her mind. Just being with him again is weakening her resolve. *Why can't I think straight, like last night*? Even if she were to try to explain to him, what she had resolved in her mind last night, it would be pointless.

She knows he still cares for her, as a friend. They will always have those childhood memories, no matter what. It would probably only make him feel sad for her, if she were to tell him everything. It would be selfish on her part, serve no good purpose. Darel is lost to her, just as Binda is, she reminds herself.

But, she feels her emotions rising up, taunting her mind. It would be so good to be able to let her guard down, tell him how much she missed sitting with him here by the river, talking with him, listening to his stories. She wants to let him know that she could always sense his presence, even when he was hundreds of kilometres away. Would he understand if she were to say, knowing he was here had made her feel that Binda was never truly lost to her? But, having said those things she would be unable to stop there. It would spill from her lips that somewhere between their childhood and adult years, her feelings had grown stronger, different, towards him. Whereas she had once hugged him with loving friendship, she now ached for him to touch her tenderly, hold her firmly and kiss her passionately.

No, she can't tell him these things now, *it's too late*. She knows Darel still feels sorry for her that she lost her family home. She doesn't want him to feel sad when he thinks about her. And if he were to think, for just one second, she was pretending these feelings for him, to try to make him fall in love with her so she could return to Binda, she would be devastated.

It doesn't matter now though, even if she did come clean. Darel has already chosen Grace. Rachel would never be Binda's mistress, but more importantly, she would never be Darel's wife. And, like a blindfold being removed from her eyes, it is only right at this very moment that she sees the truth of why she pined for Binda so much, for so many years.

"Yes. It's time to move on." She nearly chokes on her words.

"You won't be happy Rach. I *know* you."

Rachel reacts instantly. "You can say whatever you want Darel, but you can't predict my future. We both need to stop feeling sad about the past. Yes, only you know how much I love... Binda, but I need to – let go."

"Then tell me honestly Rach. Do you love Martin? Tell me the truth."

Why did he have to ask her that, now? Just when she realised with full certainty that if she couldn't have Darel, then she didn't' want anyone; that she was going to break it off with Martin. She immediately thinks of Darel with Grace, and it feels like a knife slicing her heart.

Be strong Rachel. "That's none of your business. I have to go."

No longer able to hold back the tears, she jumps up from

the log, and races towards the Corolla. She gets into her car, but as she pulls the door closed behind her, Darel is already at the window.

"Rach...I'm sorry. Please, don't go." He looks at her, pain etched across his face.

"Don't you see Darel? I have to. I once had two true loves, and now I don't have either..." she implores with her eyes, tears spilling down her cheeks "...because, by the time I realised the one I *thought* I loved the most was meaningless without the love from the other, it was too late." She blurts out and winces.

Darel's face contorts with confusion, and he pleads for understanding, "Rach, I don't understand what you mean?"

Darel's words stab at her heart. She can't leave him like this, the image of his torment etched in her mind. She somehow finds the courage to make it clear. "Darel, I have always loved you, but I thought it was because of my love for Binda. It took a while for me to work out that my love for Binda is because of *you*. I know I have no right to say that now, because of Grace."

His face instantly relaxes, but there is still some confusion lingering. "Rach, you spoke to Grace earlier, did she tell you...?"

"She didn't need to tell me Darel. It's perfectly clear that she has your heart; that she will end up as your wife. Just like your mother ended up marrying your father after she came to live with him. It's now obvious, it was never meant to be me." A loud sob escapes from her lips as she turns the ignition key, causing the Corolla to roar to life. With her eyes ahead, she tears down the track, leaving dust in its wake,

Darel finally manages to respond. "Rach, Grace is my ....half-sister," he exclaims, dumbfounded. "And, I have always been - *yours*," he groans softly.

CHAPTER 18

Rachel struggles to see the track in front of her because she is nearly blinded by the tears cascading from her eyes.

"Stupid, stupid, stupid," she bullies herself, out loud. "What an idiot you are Rachel Winton."

She practically flies past the homestead, grateful that the dogs are nowhere to be seen. She doesn't want to be responsible for running over one of them. She knows she should slow down, but she just wants to get away from Binda now, as quickly as possible. *Well, you wanted to say goodbye. You sure made it clear, even if it wasn't how you expected.*

She approaches the front gate and taps the brake, though still travelling a little too fast to turn the vehicle to the right after the gate, and onto the road, comfortably. As she passes through the gate, she plants her foot more firmly on the brake, while turning the wheel to the right. The car skids on the gravel, and comes to a sudden stop on the other side of the road, a few centimetres from the trunk of a large tree.

"Oh, damn, I really need this at the moment," she groans. The shock of the near accident forces her to reclaim her self-control. She attempts to start the engine again, but it won't kick over. And just as she is about to try again, she hears a motor bike coming towards her, from the direction of Binda.

Darel comes into view a few seconds later, at the gate. He crosses the road, turns off the engine, and races towards Rachel as she alights from the car.

"Are you alright," he says grabbing her by the forearms, with panic in his eyes.

"Yes, I'm fine Darel." She disengages herself from his grip, leans back against the side of the car and crosses her arms. "I'm sorry," she says softly, looking down at the ground.

She can feel him looking at her, but she refuses to look at him. "You should be too," he says, lifting her chin with his finger, to look into her eyes. "You scared the living daylight's outta me taking off like that."

"I know. It was *stupid*." She turns to remove his touch again, and looks into the car. "I can't start it now. Have I broken it, do you think?" she asks seriously.

Despite his recent concern, he chuckles softly. "I'm sure it will be fine. Let's have a look."

He attempts to start the car without success, so he pops the bonnet to check the engine.

"It's been making a tapping noise for a while now. I was supposed to get it looked at, she confesses, looking guilty.

He looks up from the engine at her, as if contemplating something. "Ahh, well perhaps she could do with a rest overnight at Binda. I'll have a good look at her in the mornin'." He looks at her for her answer.

"*Tomorrow!* But, I can't stay here tonight."

"Why not, there's plenty of room? And I know you're a good camper. I could even put up a tent for you if you want." He grins.

"But Darel, I can't stay..." She's debating about asking him for a lift into town, but then she would still need to get a lift back out to collect her car.

Darel decides he's stirred her enough. "Rach, I need to show you something. I'll come down and tow your car back to the shed in a bit. Come on." He walks to the motor bike, but Rachel is still standing by her car, looking annoyed.

He starts the motor bike, and ignoring her crossed arms and the frown on her face, he taps the seat behind him, indicating that he wants her to get on.

Rachel knows she has no other choice. She can't just stand here beside a car that won't start. She leans in and grabs her shoulder bag from the car, placing the long strap across her upper body, and walks to the side of the motor bike. She's glad at least that she decided to wear jeans today. Darel shows her where to put her feet and places her arms around his body.

"Hold on tight. Ok?"

She nods, and they slowly cross the road, and through the front gates of Binda. As they're travelling up the front drive, she closes her eyes and savours the moment. It will be the last time she'll ever be this close to him. She wriggles forward, closer to his body and rests her head on his back. *I don't know what he wants to show me, but right at this moment, I don't care.*

She feels the motor bike start to slow and opens her eyes. They have arrived at the house. Grace is standing out the front. She moves further back in the seat, and unlocks her fingers so that she is no longer encircling his waist, but only holding his sides, gently.

Grace has a concerned look on her face. "Everything alright?" she asks Darel, as he pulls to a stop beside her, the motor still purring.

"Yep. We've got a visitor for the night. Be back soon," he says. Grace nods and smiles at Rachel. Rachel decides she really must get her manners back at least. Besides, Grace has a lovely smile and it seems sincere. She smiles back tentatively as Darel grabs her hands and pulls them to interlock in front of him again, and takes off along the track to the river.

As they're heading back to the spot where she met him earlier, she's thinking about their previous conversation.

She's feeling embarrassed by some of the things she recalls saying to him, and yet, she now also feels strangely liberated. Another of her favourite quotes comes to mind; *'The truth shall set you free.'* Well, she ended up telling him the truth, and it will set them both free.

At least Darel now knows that her love for Binda was because of her love for him. And she knows that he has always cared about her, at least. He's proven that today. She'll need to tell him that now, when they pull up; let him know that she wants him to be happy. He is right too, about Martin. He wouldn't be able to make her happy, and it wouldn't have been fair to him either, to continue their relationship. But, how does he know about Martin, anyway, besides seeing him at the B & S Ball? How does he even know his name?

The motor bike comes to a stop. She dismounts and waits for him to do the same. He grabs her hand and is just about to head off in the direction of the dividing fence, when he stops and diverts to the log they had been sitting on earlier, instead. He sits down, pulling her to sit beside him.

"You said you wanted to show me something?" she asks, noticing that he is still holding her hand.

"Yep, but not just yet, ok?" He lets go of her hand and rests both his hands on his drawn up knees.

"Okay….Darel, I want you to know…" she begins, but is

quickly cut off.

"Rach, Grace is my sister," he says abruptly, and waits for her reaction. Rachel freezes, unable to respond, so he continues..."I tried to introduce you to her last night...," he begins, but doesn't say anything else, allowing Rachel to fully absorb it.

"But... that doesn't make sense Darel. How...when...," she finally says, frowning in confusion.

"Well, she's really my half-sister, but as far as I'm concerned, she's still my sister."

"Oh, so your mother must have been married before..."

"No, she wasn't married," he looks at her, and she notices his eyes becoming moist.

She is still trying to collect her thoughts – *his sister*! She suddenly feels drawn to move closer to him. She can see that he is finding it difficult to think about whatever it is he wants to tell her. She wants to give him some support.

"Remember what I told you about Mum being taken away from her family?" He watches her nod her head. "Well, that wasn't the only thing that made her so sad," he says, looking momentarily at the river, and then back to her. "She was ... taken advantage of, by a white man, at a property called Barons Reach, where she worked before coming to Jannali. And just before she came here, she had a baby girl. Grace."

Rachel stares at Darel, trying to absorb the information.

He continues. "Grace was adopted by a white family in the Bathurst area. The church organised it, and even named her, Grace. Her adoptive mother told her about it when she was about ten, after their miracle 'natural' child came along. She said the Church named her Grace, because it would only be by the grace of God that she would be adopted into a good Christian family."

"Oh Darel, that's so sad," she suddenly says softly, her own eyes now moist with tears.

He reaches over and holds her hand. She squeezes it gently, encouraging him, knowing there is more he wants to say. "She said she was treated well at first, because she looked white. Her parents were the only ones who knew her mother was part-aboriginal, besides the church and the people at Baron's Reach. But things were never the same for her once her younger sister was born. By the time we met her, she was living on her own in a small flat in Bathurst, and working at the hospital, in the office area. Admin..., I think she called it."

"How did you find her?"

"She found, *us*. Mum received a letter from her. I didn't know about her until then."

Rachel recalls the conversation she had with her father about aborigines when they were still at Binda. To think, Grace was going through something like that at the time.

Darel continues…,"Because of her work at the hospital, she had access to all the records there. She did a bit of searching, to see if she could find out anything more than what her adoptive mother had told her. All she knew was what she had been told; that her mother had been part-aboriginal, and had worked as a domestic in the bush somewhere. But, she remembered watching her adoptive mother putting her baby sister's hospital band in a box in a cupboard when she came home from the hospital. She had been curious and later sneaked back to look in the box, and found another one, exactly the same, with her name on it. That memory was what had prompted her to search the hospital records. She figured she must have been taken to hospital to be checked out as part of the adoption process. Anyway, she found her record, and saw that Baron's Reach was listed as 'place of birth', and Mary Gilmour, her mother.

"Oh poor Grace," Rachel interrupts. "Just imagine what must have been going through her mind. So, how did she finally find your mother at Jannali?"

"Well, she found out at Barons Reach. She drove out there and spoke to the mistress of the house. She said she was trying to track down Mary Gilmour; that she knew she had once worked for her. Apparently, the old lady wasn't very helpful at first, seemed to get all defensive the moment she had mentioned Mum's name. She told Grace to leave.

Grace knew she had to leave, but while she had been talking to the old lady she had noticed her holding on to a big gold cross that hung around her neck. She was banking on the old lady being a strict Christian, a regular church goer. So she told her, "I'll leave, but I'll tell you this first. I won't ever stop looking for my mother. If you won't tell me, I'll stand at the door of every church in Bathurst and ask if anyone knows of what happened to Mary Gilmour's baby, born at Barons Reach. I'd best be prepared, if I were you, for the news to reach you, from 'well-meaning' friends. And then she turned to leave.

"Wow, go Grace," Rachel says, impressed.

Darel smiles because of her words, and Rachel is happy to see it. "Yeah, she reminds me a lot of someone else I know."

"So...?" she prompts him, squeezing his hand and smiling briefly to acknowledge his last words.

"Well, just as she reached the door, the old lady told her to wait. She then told her that Mum had left shortly after Grace was born, to work for the Rutherfords at Dubbo. After checking the telephone directory, she found our property name beside the only Rutherfords still listed from these parts. She posted a letter asking for information." He chuckles. "You should have seen the look on Mum's face when she had finished reading the letter. I'll never forget it,

Rach," he says, looking away into the distance, remembering.

Rachel takes a deep breath and looks at Darel, shaking her head from side to side in disbelief. "When did this all happen?"

"The beginning of this year. It took a few months for it to all sink in, on both sides, I think. There was a mixture of sadness as well as happiness, at first. But after a few meetings, Mum asked Grace if she would like to move to Jannali, so she could see more of us. Well, Mum was over the moon when she turned up with her suitcases a few weeks later, after quitting her job and moving out of her flat in Bathurst. She has been with us ever since, although she still plans on finding a job at Dubbo and living there.

"So, she's now living at Binda, with you?"

Darel looks at her intently as he says his next words, hoping to gauge her feelings about it. "Yeah, we moved into the house a few months after Grace arrived." She nods, and seems to be ok about it, so he continues. "I've been working with Dad full-time since I left Dubbo High, nearly three years ago now."

"Yeah, I overheard Mum and Dad talking about how you had finished up at Dubbo High after getting your School Certificate. That was a few days after the last time I saw you that summer" She looks around her, remembering. They had been sitting on this very same log.

Darel notices her mind drifting, so he continues quickly, wanting to finish telling her about why he and Grace are living in her old home. "Well, after Grace turned up, Dad told me that one of the reasons he bought Binda from your father was so I could have a place of my own one day, while he and Mum were still around. Then when they pass on, Jannali and Binda would both be mine, side by side. He said he was going to suggest I move out to Binda when I turned twenty-one or got married, whichever came sooner." He notices Rachel avoiding his eyes. "But even though I was still only eighteen when Grace turned up, he said I could move in sooner if I wanted to, with Grace. He said that way she wouldn't feel she had to move to Dubbo in a hurry, give her something to do, and it would help me with the cooking and everything. She still sees Mum every day, either at Binda or Jannali. The tracks you and I used are well-worn by both of them." He pauses to see that she smiles at his last comment.

"Anyway, I think they're hoping I'll help her get to know the area, and people, too."

"So, that's why you're both in the tennis comp. As partners," Rachel asks.

He nods. "She still intends moving into Dubbo, when she finds more work there. She wants to get to know people too. By the way, you're pretty alright with a racquet in your hand," he says, grinning.

Rachel blushes slightly. "And *you*, too. I know now why you got the nickname, Ace."

They both become quiet, lost in their thoughts for the moment.

"I'm really glad Grace found her mother, and you. And, although I know you may not believe me, I *am* happy you're living at Binda. I'm sorry I acted so crazy earlier."

Darel moves closer to Rachel and puts his arm around her. He looks into her eyes. "I believe you Rach, and it's ok."

He stands up and holds his hands out for her to take, and pulls her up when she does. "I know I said there was something I wanted to show you, but I'd rather wait until tomorrow now. It's getting late, and I need to pack up here. Can you give me a hand, drive the ute back to the house for me? Then we'll go get your car, ok?"

She nods. "Ok, but I better ring home and tell them I'm here. They'll worry if I don't show up. I told Dad I was only going for a drive."

CHAPTER 19

"I'll be home tomorrow sometime Dad. See ya then." Rachel hangs up the phone with a deep sigh. She was relieved her father had answered the phone. Although she had expected both her parents to be disappointed in her for nearly totalling her car, her father had obviously been more concerned that she had not been hurt. Her mother would have been concerned about her too, but that would have been a conversation riddled with multiple questions, leaving her feeling much worse.

She suddenly feels drained. It has been a huge day. She can feel a headache coming on. Something about Martin keeps trying to enter her thoughts, but with having to take in so much about Darel and Grace, she doesn't want to dwell on it, so she keeps pushing it away.

As she walks into the kitchen, after using the phone in the hall, she notices Grace washing up and glances around for a tea towel.

"No you don't," Grace admonishes her. "You go on out and enjoy the sunset. It's really beautiful from the verandah, as you would know," she adds, with a smile. "Darel just had to go do something, so I thought I'd get these out of the way while you were on the phone. I'm nearly done, so off you go. Oh, and Darel said to tell you he'll be back soon."

Rachel does as she is told and walks out to the verandah. She settles herself into the soft pastel cushion of a wicker chair, and gazes towards the river.

The pink hues are slowly spreading across the sky, as the sun dips behind the river gums. Tiny sparkles of water flicker in between the branches. She thinks about how so much has changed in so short a time.

When she had first arrived at Binda, she thought she would be saying goodbye to Darel, forever. But, now she knows about Grace, and Darel knows how she feels about him...? Well, she still needs to keep her emotions in check. She doesn't know if he feels exactly the same way. And, regardless, she doesn't want to lose his friendship, no matter what. If she hadn't driven off like a lunatic, she imagines she would most likely be back at Dubbo, nursing a broken heart, and feeling like a fool. Sometimes it's very strange the way things happen, she muses.

At the river, Darel had loaded the ute with the fencing gear, and placed the esky and thermos into the passenger seat beside her. She had then followed him as he slowly rode the motor bike along the track to the house, skilfully avoiding any potholes or fallen branches.

When they had arrived at the house, Darel had parked the motor bike and removed the esky and thermos from the passenger seat of the ute. He had then taken Rachel back to her car. She had sat in the driver's seat of the Corolla, keeping the steering wheel straight, while he had towed it back to the shed. Grace had come out shortly after and they had all come inside for tea.

She had followed Grace through the front door, smiling, determined to keep a cheerful look on her face, despite feeling apprehensive. She was still unsure how she would feel about seeing different furnishing and belongings in her old home.

"Make yourself at home Rachel. Please," Grace had said sincerely, pausing by the lounge room door. She had looked past her to Darel, and he had nodded, so she had continued, "I mean it, and as far as Darel and I are concerned, it's still your home."

Rachel had instantly felt welcome. As she followed Grace into the lounge room, she was also very surprised to find that she immediately liked the differences she saw. Although the furnishings were much sparser than they had been when she had lived there, the more modern style of the lounge room gave the place a much fresher feel.

The bulky oak and floral pattered lounge suite and recliner seats in the lounge room had been replaced with a turquoise coloured three-seater sofa and two matching armchairs. Turquoise was her favourite colour, and when she had turned to look at Darel after appraising it, she had noted an understanding smile on his face.

Where the piano had once stood, there was now a television set, tucked into a teak entertainment unit. The old bookcase still stood along the opposite wall to the door they had walked through. Although comparatively small, it had been unmovable, due to it originally being built into the wall, so it had remained in the house. It was now looking a little bare overall: obvious gaps where a set of encyclopaedia and an assortment of older books once nestled. However, there were some books strategically placed in the centre, around which were assembled, an assortment of interesting things.

There was a piece of quartz crystal and several smaller different coloured stones in one section; an assortment of bottles of different shapes and colours in another; and looking up higher, she saw two matching dark green vases decorated beautifully with scenes of the Australian bush. Just as she was about to turn her gaze away, she looked back to the centre of the bookcase and recognised the books displayed there. She had immediately looked at Darel.

"Yeah, of course I still have them. I like their shape, remember?" he says grinning.

Grace had prepared a simple but enjoyable meal for them

of leftover roast leg of lamb smothered in gravy, perfectly cooked potatoes, carrots and peas, topped off by rice custard and tinned peaches, for dessert.

As they began their meal, Rachel realised she was feeling relaxed for the first time all day, although a little unsure about making conversation with Grace. How much was she supposed to know about her? Would it be rude to ask her questions, and if she didn't, would that seem rude as well? Darel had looked her way as these thoughts had been going through her mind, and he had seemed to know.

"Grace, I told Rachel everything about you," he said bluntly.

Rachel looked up quickly, to gauge Grace's reaction.

"Oh good, now we have that over and done with... Rachel, is there much admin work available in Dubbo, do you think? Where's the best place to look?"

Rachel had breathed deeply then, and from that moment conversation had flowed easily and freely between the three of them. She had literally felt her muscles relax, and when she next looked up from her plate, she had looked directly into Grace's eyes, and saw something in their expression that caused her to voice her thoughts.

"You have the same eyes as your mother."

Grace and Darel had both smiled then, first at each other, and then at her.

"Yeah, she does," Darel confirms. "Mum and Grace also worked out that she has exactly the same coloured hair too, although Grace's is long and more wavy, and not as..," he concentrates trying to think of the word.

"Wispy," Grace answers for him.

"Yeah, not as wispy as Mum's. Whatever that means. Anyway, they're both good-lookers," Darel had said, rolling his eyes with a cheeky look on his face.

Grace had then picked up a pea from her plate and thrown it at Darel, laughing, and he had pretended to be shocked. Rachel had laughed also, and watching the friendly banter between them, she noted how alike they were in some of their ways.

Yes, this day has ended up far better than I expected. She wonders though, if she'll be able to sleep tonight, knowing that Darel will be close by in another room.

As she had walked down the hallway to the bathroom earlier, she had found it too difficult to avoid looking through the open doors of the bedrooms. It was obvious that Darel slept in the main bedroom. It was a little untidy with a pair of boots lying where they had been thrown in the corner, a pair of jeans and a belt across a chair, and bits and pieces strewn across the dressing table area, another built-in feature of the 1950's styled house.

Grace no doubt, now occupied what was called the third,

or spare, bedroom, when Rachel had lived there. There was a suitcase and several other carry bags and small boxes positioned along the wall near a dresser, upon which stood a mirror, bush and comb set, a small silver jewellery box and an assortment of hair clasps.

Her old bedroom was the only room left completely bare, except for a white based, unmade single bed and matching dressing table. Perhaps she should ask Grace for some bedding to make up her bed. She feels she should be doing something. Obviously Darel is busy somewhere. Where is he anyway? He said at tea that he would look at her car in the morning, so he wouldn't be doing that.

As if hearing her inner conversation, Darel immediately appears from around the side of the house and walks up the steps to join her. He sits down beside her in another wicker chair and looks out at the sunset.

"Not a bad view from here, hey?"

"I reckon," she replies with a grin.

"Be better by the river though, don't you think?"

"Of course...." She was about to say, "Let's go check it out," but it will soon be dark and she imagines he's probably not far off going to bed, having obviously been fencing for most of the day.

"Well," he says, standing up and holding out his hand to her. "We'd best make tracks. Everything we need is in the ute. We'll say goodnight to Grace on the way out. C'mon Rach, we're camping by the river tonight" he says smiling broadly.

CHAPTER 20

"So, this is what you were doing," she says excitedly, looking at the three man tent positioned a short distance from their favourite log.

He smiles, seeing her approval. "Well, I know you love camping," he says as he bends down near the fire close by.

Rachel looks at him kneeling on the ground, attending to the fire. She goes over to the tent and looks in. There are two sleeping bags side by side, one on top of several thick blankets.

He joins her, looking into the tent, and motions to the sleeping bag with the additional blankets underneath. "Well, I know you can rough it, but you're *my* guest, and I want you to be comfortable."

He then points to the corner of the tent. "There's another blanket there too, and a few extra things including some towels, drinking water, marshmallows and some fruit. Oh, and a roll of toilet paper for you, in case you need it." She blushes and he grins.

"Well thank you kind sir," she says playfully. "No, seriously, thank you. It's really great." She reaches out, about to give him a hug, but stops herself.

He notices her hesitate, so turns and walks back over to the fire, saying over his shoulder, "You're welcome Rach, come sit down, we have nearly three years to catch up on."

Over the next few hours, as they watch the sun completely set before their eyes, and listen to the nocturnal sounds surfacing, they talk about the last few years.

Rachel tells him about her last two years at Trinity; the activities she undertook for the Gold award, Duke of Edinburgh and even about her few months of rebellion.

"Well, it helped to get Mum off my back about going to uni. I dunno Darel, I just couldn't go any further than Dubbo, not after Trinity. It was like I was tied with a rope, anchored to the district. I don't think I would have been able to leave even if I had wanted to. That make sense?"

"Yep, I know what you're sayin'. I couldn't live anywhere else either. And I can't think of anything I'd rather do than care for this land like I am." He then tells her what he's been doing around the properties, both with his father and by himself.

"You work hard. I guess that's why you don't get into Dubbo much."

"More than you think, especially this year," he says with a grin.

"Why?" she asks, tentatively.

"Well, usually I go to town a bit during cricket season, and lately, tennis. But I also started going into Wallis & Co this year. Dad usually does it." He waits expectantly for any response.

"Ahh, yes," she smiles. "Well, it seems to me that someone keeps coming in there at the wrong time."

"Don't I know it? Are you sure you work there?" he teases.

She picks up a pebble and throws it at him playfully. "Well, I'm sorry I kept missing you. Didn't Dad tell you I'm only there in the afternoons, till the end of this year? I'll be there full-time after that."

"Well, I didn't want to ask too much about you, after what your mother said, so I was just hoping to chance you being there."

Rachel immediately stops drawing shapes in the dirt with a twig she had picked up. "What do you mean, what my mother said?" She feels her blood pressure start to rise.

"Well, I was at the store, a few months ago. Your mother was there, alone. I don't know where your father was. I guess you were still at TAFE. Anyway, we talked a bit about Binda and Jannali, and then as I was leaving, I asked her if she would let you know I had been there."

"Was this after I saw you the first time there?" Rachel asks.

"Yeah. Anyway, as soon as I said that, she started talking about Martin. She said you had been together since Trinity, and that although you weren't in Canberra with him now, you would be in the future. She even told me he was going to be with you at the B and S Ball."

Rachel hurls the stick into the fire, and drops her head into her hands, in exasperation. "Ahhh, I wish she would keep her nose out of my business. I really need to find my own place." She then looks up to Darel. "Now I know how you know his name. Even since you mentioned it earlier today, I've been wondering."

Darel looks at her thoughtfully, and she knows what he's thinking.

"It's over between Martin and I, Darel. I just have to tell him."

He nods seriously, and then jumps up and announces as if inspired, "Toasted marshmallows are in order, I think."

Later, after they have had their fill of warm, sticky marshmallows they had roasted on long prong forks over the hot coals of the fire, Rachel and Darel sit with their backs resting up against the log, staring into the fire in front of them. She lifts her arm and pats the log with her hand.

"This log could tell so many stories," she says. "It's been here forever, or at least all our lives, hey?"

"Yep, sure has. Just like most of these trees," he answers

as he looks around at the river gums, and the shadowed patterns from the fire, dancing on their trunks.

Rachel looks up to the stars and the moon. "I was thinking about the dreaming of Mirrabooka last night, after tennis."

"Were you? You still remember the stories?"

"Oh yes. I've never forgotten them Darel." *I've never forgotten anything to do with you.* She decides to confess. "I wrote them down in a diary. I'm sorry, I know you probably didn't want me to do that, because they were supposed to be a secret. Someone read my diary too." She looks at him with obvious regret.

"It's ok Rach," he says moving closer to her. "It doesn't matter now. Mum feels safe. She knows no-one can hurt her anymore."

"Oh, that's a huge relief. I felt so guilty about it, for so long." She then mimics herself as a younger version, "I keep my promises."

"Ha. You've always had that spark," he says, looking at her proudly. He looks at the fire, and then back to her. "You know more than Grace too, about the Wiradjuri people," he says, and nods when she opens her eyes wide in surprise. "Remember, she grew up with white parents."

"Then you'll have to teach her too," she says with conviction. "That's what it's all about, isn't it? To ensure that everything about your mother's people is never forgotten?"

He nods, and they both look up to the sky together.

"I was looking at the moon last night too, driving home, and..." He stops and turns to look at her directly. "Did you really mean what you said earlier today Rach? I need to know."

She turns to him and looks into his eyes. "Yes Darel, I meant every word of it, but... I don't want to lose your friendship, even if you don't feel the same." There, she had said it. She had yet again, opened up her heart to him. She could do no more. She watches him watching her and he's now looking at her like he had last night in the tennis club. "Why are you looking at me that way," she says softly.

He positions himself closer to her and placing both hands either side of her face, he leans in and kisses her. He kisses her hesitantly, caressing each section of her lips with his own, in gentle reverence.

"You have the most beautiful lips, Rachel Elizabeth Winton," he says, as if to reassure her that he is thinking only of her.

"I won't break, Darel William Rutherford," she says in serious response.

He leans over her, pushing her head and shoulders firmly against his arm that he has placed behind her on the top of the log. He closes his mouth over hers and kisses her hungrily, teasing her on and off by lifting away to look deeply into her eyes, before returning again to savour the sweetness of her lips.

Rachel feels his arms around her, his mouth on hers, and looks deeply into his eyes when he draws back to look into her soul. She doesn't need to hear the words he now says, to know.

"I love you Rach, always have, always will. Don't ever forget that."

She can't stop the tears that surface, nor does she want to. She feels them moving through her body like water in a river, flowing into every part of her body, replenishing, healing.

"Please don't cry," he says, his eyes beginning to grow moist. "I can't stand to see you cry," he says softly.

"It's ok," she whispers. "They're not deep water tears. They are tears of joy!"

EPILOGUE

Rachel pauses to look at the engraving, as she navigates the track between the river bank and the old white gum. A smile lights her face. Every time she passes by it, she thinks back to the first time Darel had taken her camping, here by the river.

They had woken the following morning to a raucous chorus of kookaburra's laughing, magpies warbling and cockatoos screeching. Rachel had felt Darel's body beside hers and opened her eyes to see him gazing lovingly at her. They had walked down to the river, hand in hand, the morning sun and tender caresses, warming each other, as they bathed. Afterwards, he had said it was time to show her what he had mentioned the previous day.

He had taken her to the old white gum tree where she now stands. He had pointed to the aboriginal designs, etched into the tree, long before either of them had been born, and even longer than before any white man had ever set foot in the area. At the moment Darel had pointed, her dream had again surfaced, but this time, unlike her dream, when she looked to where he indicated, she had not only seen the original aborigine engraving, but another, newer engraving. Before she could comment, Darel had said, "I did this just after I kissed you that first time. When we were fifteen."

She had reached up and traced along the carved initials with her finger; 'D' and 'R' at the top, followed by 'and', and her initials, 'R' and 'W', ending with the universal heart shape surrounding them.

"I told you last night that I have always loved you, and always will, Rach. This engraving will be here for as long as this tree is, but my love for you will never die."

She had looked again at the engravings, and it had become clear to her then. In her dream, the faces of Grace and his mother behind him, had been to tell her they were part of him, an integral link to his past.

Laughter interrupts her nostalgia, and she looks to the source. William and Elizabeth are playing tag amongst the trees ahead of her, beside the track leading to Jannali. William turns, looks at her, and yells, "C'mon Mum."

A replica of Darel's smile beams at her as his sister with her shiny blonde hair jumps out from behind a tree and tags him. He races off after her as Rachel yells, "Coming."

She begins to walk again, but returns to her previous thoughts, as she watches her children playing ahead.

Darel had found the problem with her car and repaired it later that morning. She can't remember what the problem had been, but she had no longer heard a tapping noise after that.

Later that day, she had driven to Dubbo and found both her parents in the kitchen, having afternoon tea. Her mother had begun to rant as soon as she walked through the door.

"Why did it take you so long to get home, and why did you go to Binda in the first place Rachel...?" But, she had stopped her short.

"Mum, Darel and I will be seeing a great deal of each other from now on. And I'll be moving out as soon as I find a suitable place to rent."

Her mother had gasped, "But what about Martin?"

Her father had patted Betty's hand patronisingly. "Dear, I think Rachel's just told us. We may as well get used to the idea." He had then looked at Rachel with a grin, and winked.

That night, she had phoned Jess at the Chinese restaurant, where she worked, and then Martin at the university hostel. Neither of them had seemed their usual selves, but they had both seemed a little relieved to know she was coming to Canberra the following weekend. Rachel had wondered if they somehow already knew what she was going to tell them.

She had found out soon enough. They were together in Martin's room when she arrived. At first she had been concerned by the looks on their faces, wondering if something terrible had happened. But once they begin talking she couldn't have been more relieved.

Ever since Martin had taken Jess up on her suggestion to visit the Chinese restaurant where she worked part-time, they had been spending a lot of time together. At first, they both thought it was just friendship, a mutual connection through Rachel. But one night, when they had met up for a night out with several other friends, they had realised it was much more. They had both felt riddled with guilt and had been planning on coming to Dubbo to tell Rachel in person. When Rachel told them about Darel, they all hugged and vowed that nothing would ever get in the way of their friendship.

When she had thought about Jess and Martin as a couple, on her way back to Dubbo, she realised the signs had always been there; even since Trinity. Why had Jess pushed her towards Martin? Because she had noticed the way he had looked at Rachel, even though he had never noticed the way Jess had looked at him.

Rachel then understood how hard it must have been for Jess. Yet, she hadn't allowed herself to let Martin know her feelings, until Darel had re-entered Rachel's life.

They were married now. Jess had become a counsellor after finishing university, and Martin, an accountant. They were both living and working in Canberra. They had decided not to start a family yet, unlike Rachel and Darel.

She had moved out to her own flat shortly after she told

her parents about Darel. It had given her the sense of independence she had needed. Most of her weekends had then been spent at Binda with Darel, and he had seemed to find more excuses to come to town during the week as well. She completed her secretarial studies at TAFE, and continued to work full-time at Wallis and Co, until the end of January 1981.

Grace had found an administration job at the medical centre in Dubbo; her previous experience working at Bathurst Hospital, a decided advantage at her interview for the position. She had then moved into the spare room in Rachel's flat. It had worked out so well.

At first, when Jess came to visit, the three women would sit around talking and laughing, and sometimes go out on a girl's night out. Grace was almost five years older than they both were, but that didn't stop her from knowing how to have a good time. Sometimes Darel, Johno and Martin would join the three girls. Grace even found Johno fun to be around, although it never eventuated into anything more. Grace eventually found her soul-mate, but that's another story...

Rachel thinks briefly of her own marriage to Darel, almost eight years ago now. They had both turned twenty-one near the beginning of that year; January 19th for Darel and March 9th for Rachel. They had decided that February, the month between their birthdays, would be ideal for two reasons. The summer months had always been their favourite time of the year, when in the evening the river water still shimmered from the warmth of the sun, and in 1981; Saturday, February 14th, fell on Valentine's Day. They couldn't think of a more perfect date.

So, they were married at their favourite meeting spot by the river at Binda, surrounded by their family and friends. The sun set as vows were exchanged and as they kissed to seal their union, the kookaburras broke out in glorious laughter, and Mary Rutherford joined them. That night, after the wedding celebrations back at Binda, they stole away into the night on their honeymoon; their destination, the Warrumbungle National Park.

"I keep my promises too, Rach," Darel had said.

Rachel catches up to her children as they reach the Jannali homestead. She calls to seven-year-old William and five-year-old Elizabeth, and they race back to her.

"Don't forget Will, you wanted me to remind you to ask Grandma Mary about those wiggly marks on the tree."

"Oh yeah, thanks Mum," William says, as his eyes grow wide and he turns to run ahead again to the homestead.

"Me too, me too," Elizabeth yells, spurting off behind him, almost tripping over a branch.

"Careful now Libby," Rachel calls.

Just then, Darel turns the corner of the house, and grabs the children. They shriek with delight. He lets them go and they continue around the corner of the house to see Grandma Mary and Grandpa Don.

Darel waits for Rachel. She walks up to him and he pulls her firmly against him and looks deeply into her eyes. No words are necessary.

Coming Soon...

Grace
Book 2
The Dreaming Series

www.ingramcontent.com/pod-product-compliance
Lightning Source LLC
Chambersburg PA
CBHW020554180626
46810CB00007B/2495